THE WEATHER IN KANSAS: SHORT STORIES

CRISTA ERMIYA

RED SQUIRREL PRESS

First published in the UK in 2015 by Red Squirrel Press
www.redsquirrelpress.com

Reprinted 2016

Red Squirrel Press is distributed by Central Books Ltd.
Represented by Inpress Books Ltd.
www.redsquirrelpress.com

A CIP catalogue is available from the British Library.

ISBN: 978 1 906700 997

Printed by Charlesworth Press

For Dave and Alex, with love

Contents

1977

Memet Ali was eight years old when a woman on his estate gave birth to a cockerel. Elif. He remembered that her name was Elif.

Elif wasn't exactly pretty, as such. She had a long torso and short legs, so that when she sat down, paradoxically she looked taller. Her hair was dark, thick and long with a slight kink to it that made it easier for tendrils to escape from under her headscarf. The skin on her face was lightly pockmarked on one cheek where she had scratched at chicken pox spots when she was eleven. Her almost-black eyes were large and set slightly too wide apart. Some of the other Turks on the estate, including Memet Ali's grandmother, said they were the eyes of a woman who saw djinn. Despite these superficial flaws that edged her otherwise ordinary prettiness towards the plain, Elif had acquired the unwanted status of local siren. Although never fully articulated by the neighbours, the reason for this was unfairly straightforward: at the age of nineteen, Elif was already a widow.

She had arrived two years previously, hair wrapped in a scarf, legs encased in stiff indigo jeans, with a permanent shiver that sent the heating bills through the roof. At first everyone assumed she was Suleyman's niece, or even an illegitimate daughter. It was a couple of weeks before he admitted that she was his new wife.

Those who were so inclined sucked their teeth. Memet Ali's father restricted himself to a mutter, "that is not the modern thing to do." Mr Ali stubbed out his cigarettes in a metal union flag ashtray, and he insisted his family eat their dinner off plasticized place-mats adorned with the St Andrew's Cross because when he was younger and newly arrived someone had told him he looked like a Hebridean fisherman with a suntan. "But then," Mr Ali said, on the subject of Suleyman's folly, "what else can you expect from a Turk?"

Suleyman was from Anatolia, whereas most of the other Turks on the estate were from Cyprus. With other personalities this wouldn't perhaps have been a big deal, but Suleyman was a naturally conservative man, and although only slightly more than perfunctorily religious, he didn't drink alcohol, even when it wasn't Ramadan. Memet was afraid of him, because whenever they came across him in the street, Suleyman would start talking to his father, loudly, about whether Mr Ali would have Memet circumcised at the appropriate age. Mr Ali didn't appreciate these extempore lectures from Suleyman, but he still insisted that Memet call the elder man Uncle Suleyman.

The neighbours were at first surprised (later transforming into malicious glee) when, a few weeks after Suleyman had returned from an extended visit to Anatolia in celebration of his fiftieth birthday, he came home one day with a teenage girl in the back of his cab, obviously just off the plane, and clutching a small vinyl suitcase to her skinny breast. Her wide-set eyes stared around at the estate unblinking, like a shocked kitten recently displaced from its litter. Memet was standing opposite, by one of the communal metal bins trying to throw a small bag of rubbish over the top. Suleyman saw him but instead of calling Memet over for a random harangue, as he would normally do, he pretended not to see the curious boy. Nor did he appear to notice the women leaning over their balconies. He quickly ushered the stranger into his stairwell.

Elif didn't go out at first, and then when she did it was always with Suleyman. Memet longed to see her out by herself. He had taken to sitting on the bottom steps of his stairwell after school, in hope of catching a glimpse of her. He was even willing to risk Uncle Suleyman quizzing him over potential plans for circumcision and sometimes accompanied the couple to the shops on the pretence of needing to get a loaf or sugar for his grandmother. Elif didn't talk much, and Memet couldn't speak Turkish anyway, apart from a few basic phrases, so their conversation always ran along the same lines. "Nasselsen?" Elif would ask how he was. "Choc e, merci,". I'm fine thank you, Memet would dutifully reply. "Sen Nasselsen?" And she would ruffle his hair in lieu of her own reply. Uncle Suleyman smiled indulgently. "You're a good boy, Memet," he said.

A year into his marriage, Suleyman had a heart attack in his cab and died in the driver seat, his car lined up in a queue outside the controller's office. No one noticed until the three cabs in front of him had gone off on jobs and he failed to respond to the next request. The neighbours were studiously over-sympathetic – *Poor Elif, what will become of her?* – predicting gloom with voyeuristic relish. *She'll have to go back home – yes, but I hear she has no family.* Memet Ali's grandmother, more practical and less susceptible to schadenfreude, went to visit her, widow to widow. She helped Elif organise the funeral: it had taken the astute grandmother less than a minute to understand that Elif was entirely without anyone to help her from amongst Suleyman's aquaintance. The funeral was attended by members of Suleyman's mosque, his fellow mini-cab drivers and some Turks from the estate. In the following weeks, the neighbours looked out for arrivals from Turkey, for either Suleyman or Elif, but no-one came. *That's strange,* people said. *Well,* said others, *what do we really know about her? Nothing. Maybe Suleyman's family back home don't even know he's dead. How do we know she's even told them? – He was an old man, maybe he has no close relatives left – He wasn't that old – Perhaps they didn't approve of his marriage to Elif – Well, you could understand that. So young! – Suleyman wasn't that old – No, it's true, these days 50 is nothing. Strange he should have a heart attack like that, all of a sudden – Are the council going to let her stay on in the flat? – What? And my son on the waiting list these past four years? – Maybe she hasn't told the authorities about Suleyman's death either.*

One afternoon, when she was not well enough to go herself, Memet Ali's grandmother sent her grandson over to Elif with some baklava. She was on the third floor of her block and Memet, against his natural inclination to go running up to see her as fast as he could, was careful to go slowly up the stairs so as not to drop the tray of sweets. When he got there he had to knock five or six times before she answered, and even then, only after he had called out to her through the letterbox. Inside, the flat was dark, all the curtains shut against the daylight, and all the electric lights off.

"Nasselsen Elif?" Memet asked.

"I'm fine," she replied, in English. She walked into the sitting room, but Memet stood in the hallway, eyes unaccustomed to the dark after the light outside. He heard her draw the curtains and the dusty afternoon lit the room.

"Come in," she said.

He went in, put the baklava on to a low smoked glass table and stood awkwardly with his hands clasped behind his back, sweating, his elbows jutting out on either side of his body.

"Sit down, Memet," Elif said.

He sat down in an armchair upholstered in a large floral brown fabric that made his legs itch through his trousers. Elif sat down on the settee.

"Baklava." She laughed.

Memet could see nothing especially funny about the baklava. "From my grandmother," he said.

"She's very kind," Elif said. "Not everyone is."

"I can be kind to you," Memet blurted out.

"The kindness of children. That's something, I suppose," she said.

Memet couldn't think of anything to say to this, and so they both sat in silence in the room as the dusty light slowly turned to evening. Memet thought it was like watching someone fall asleep with their eyes open. He should have been bored, sitting down in a room with nothing happening, but he felt a curious happiness watching her as she sat back on the settee, her head tilted up to the ceiling, eyes open but unfocused, her lips unsmiling. She still wore a headscarf, but it looked different these days, something to do with the way she tied it, that made Memet think of the three women in *Charlie's Angels*.

"Who is your favourite Angel?" Memet asked.

Elif turned her head to look at him. She looked surprised and Memet thought, with a pang, that she had forgotten he was there.

"Everyone likes the one with the blonde hair, but I like the one with the long dark hair, the one with the hair that waves at the bottom." He wanted to say, "I like her because she looks a little bit like you," but he didn't. And then the doorbell rang. They both jolted, as if they were on a bus and the doorbell was the driver braking too quickly. His dad's voice came ringing through the letterbox.

"Memet! Are you in there?"

Elif got up and went to the door.

"Merhaba Elif," he said, and then, spying Memet who had followed her into the hallway, hissed, "where have you been? Your grandmother has been worrying."

To Elif he said, "Has he been making a nuisance of himself? I'm sorry."

"No," Elif replied. "Memet is a good boy." Suleyman's stock phrase.

"Come here son," Memet called to him. Memet reluctantly edged through the front door past Elif.

"Come again," she said, and Memet's heart lifted and he smiled, until his father said, "Yes, I'll drop by sometime," as if she had been speaking to him rather than Memet.

"Poor girl," Memet Ali's father said as they walked back home together to the grandmother. "She must be lonely."

"Maybe she needs more friends," Memet suggested, thinking of putting himself forward for the role.

"Yes," Memet's father agreed. "Friends."

"You're not going over to Elif again?" the grandmother asked Memet's dad.

"And what if I am? She needs a friend in these times."

"She has too many friends these days," Memet's grandmother said.

"I'm just being a good neighbour," he told his mother-in-law.

"No. *I'm* a good neighbour. *You* are just another man."

Memet's father slammed the door on his way out.

I've heard she likes older men. – Easier to get rid of! – Ain't that

13

the truth. The girl is sly. She just come, take the flat, take the benefit. I been here since 1963, waiting to move since 1973, the council still promising — You know what I'm saying! And all them men-friends. I hear not all them get it for free you know — yep, that girl is too clever with herself.

"Gran, what are you doing?" Memet asked.

"It's to protect our home," she said. "This keeps away the evil eye."

His grandmother was putting up a mobile with three blue glass beads hanging down from thin leather straps on the inside of the front door, with a white blob in the middle of each bead. Sort of like eyes, Memet conceded.

"What's the evil eye?"

"It can be many things Memet. Sometimes it's a look, sometimes it's a person, sometimes it's the devil himself."

"Why would the devil come here?"

"There are all sorts of unlikely places for evil to come through," Memet's grandmother said. He didn't know what she was talking about; but this was often the case.

"Mother, what is this?" Memet's dad asked when he got home. "Are we living in the dark ages? No. This is modern Great Britain in the 1970s. We are not peasants."

Memet's grandmother shuffled in the kitchen, frying blobs of mincemeat for kofte. "I promised Emine I would look after you and Memet. Let me do it my way."

Memet listened hard; neither his father nor his

14

grandmother ever mentioned his mother. But they didn't say anything further about her, and Memet's father let the talisman remain.

"We should tell Elif to get one," Memet suggested.

Neither his father nor his grandmother replied.

"No-one goes to see her now that her belly has got round," Memet said.

There was a brief silence.

"You're right, Memet," said his grandmother. "Why don't you go to see her?"

Memet's father shot her a look that Memet couldn't quite understand. She continued, "Open the top left drawer in the dresser in my bedroom. There's another… decoration… in there. Take it and give to Elif. After you've eaten your tea."

Memet, unencumbered this time by pastry sweets, ran up Elif's stairwell, so that by the time he arrived on her floor he could hear his own breathing, which had got loud in the way that it sometimes did when he was in the playground. Elif was stood in her doorway.

"You're out of breath little man," she said.

Memet panted a little until he couldn't hear himself anymore, and he reached into his pocket.

"My grandmother sent you this," he said, holding out the triumvirate of blue glass beads towards her. Elif took it from his open hand and examined the talisman in her palm.

"Yes." She nodded to herself. She continued to stand in the doorway.

"What are you doing?" Memet asked.

"Nothing," Elif said.

"You can't see anything from there," Memet advised her. "If you want to look out properly you have to look over the balcony." And he stood at the balcony wall and peered over. He was just about tall enough to do so now, and took great pride in it.

"I can see our bins from here."

Elif laughed. " Nice view," she said.

She stepped over to the wall and bent forward to lean her arms over it, shielding her protruding stomach. "Back home, none of our houses were this tall. But we could see all the way to the end of the world. Miles and miles of grass, and trees, and cotton."

"My dad says that where he grew up you could hear the sea all day, even when you were in school."

"He's from an island," Elif said. "I've never seen the ocean."

Memet was incredulous. "But even I've seen it, and I'm only little. Haven't you ever been to Southend?"

"What is that?"

"It's the seaside, *everyone* knows that."

"No. I haven't been to Southend. Even when I came

over here on the airplane I couldn't see the ocean out of the window. Except once, when the cloud cleared, I saw some mountains."

"I've never seen a mountain," Memet said, impressed.

"You could see mountains from my house," Elif said. "On the horizon, right at the edge of the world I used to think."

Memet and Elif contemplated the sight of two kids who had come out of one of the opposite blocks and were now walking round a blackened car. It had been burnt out the night before. Memet had thought it looked pretty then, like bonfire night, but then some firemen came and put it out. The fire engine was quite exciting, but Memet had seen plenty of those already.

"Elif, have you got a mummy and daddy?"

Elif shook her head.

"Do you wish Uncle Suleyman was still here?"

"I don't know," she said.

"What about you? Do you miss your mummy?"

Memet didn't want to answer this, so instead he asked her something that had been bothering him for ages. "Why is your belly so big now? Have you eaten lots and lots of baklava?"

"No," Elif laughed, but it sounded odd to Memet. Too loud, somehow, too short. "I'm going to have a baby."

"A baby? Why?"

Elif didn't say anything for a bit, and then she said, almost to herself, "It will keep me company I suppose."

"Back home, the old women told me I would never have children," she added.

"Were you naughty?" Memet asked. "Is that why they wouldn't allow you?"

Elif looked down at him through narrowed eyes.

"No, I wasn't naughty."

"Then why wouldn't they let you have children?"

"It's not like making someone stay in their room, or stopping them from having any sweets," she said. But then she continued, "You're right though. They did think I was naughty."

"Why? What did you do?"

"I didn't do anything," Elif said, looking back at the burnt-out car. "But people in the village *thought* I was doing naughty things."

"Like playing in the road when you're meant to be getting bread from the shops?"

"No, like cursing chickens so they don't lay eggs. Or looking at someone's husband and then the next day he's ill."

"How did you do that?" Memet asked. This was even more impressive than the mountains.

"I didn't!" Elif cried. "Or maybe I did, I don't know.

18

Maybe we all do things without knowing what we're doing."

The two kids down below heard Elif's cry, and looked up. They shouted rude words at her, and held up their fingers in an 'up yours' gesture.

"Be careful," an adult admonished them from an unseen window. "She's a witch, she'll put a spell on you."

"She doesn't scare me!" declared one of the kids, but the other one looked away.

"Come inside," Elif said to Memet. "I'll make you some toast."

Inside was just as it always was, dark and dusty and overheated. This time Memet sat in the kitchen while Elif made some toast under the grill, and boiled water for tea. He dipped his toast into the milky tea Elif made for him and watched the crumbs swirl around on the beige surface.

"Your tea will get cold," he said to her, imitating something his grandmother would say. Elif smiled and took a sip from her own cup.

"Would you like to see some mountains?" she asked him.

Memet was uncertain. "I can't be away too long, or Gran will get worried."

"I have some pictures from home," Elif said. "You can see the mountains in the background of some of them." She lifted herself up off the chair with a little heave and went out of the room. Memet heard a shuffling noise from what was most likely the bedroom, and then Elif returned, carrying the small navy vinyl suitcase she'd had when Memet had first seen her exit Suleyman's cab two years before.

"I've not shown these to anybody, not even your grandmother." She dusted off the bottom of the case, placed it on her lap and opened it. She took out a bundle of small square photographs, 3 by 3 inch with a white thin border and passed them over to Memet. "Wipe your hands first," she said. "I don't want tea and toast on them."

Memet wiped his hands on his trousers and mutely took the proffered photographs. They were all from Elif's wedding to Suleyman. Even to Memet's untrained eye, he could see that Elif now looked much older than she had in the photographs, even though they were only from a couple of years ago. A lot of the pictures had been taken in the evening, and Elif's wedding headdress glittered red and gold in the flashbulb. She didn't look happy, exactly, Memet wouldn't say that, but there was a look in her face that she didn't have now, sitting opposite him.

"Hope," Elif said, suddenly. "I had so much hope." Memet looked at her and noticed, with a child's acuity, the fine lines developing around her dark eyes, which had acquired a sunken look as if they were being sucked back into her face. It was the kind of look his mother had when she had been vomiting.

"Where are the mountains?" he asked. Elif shuffled through the pictures until she found one.

"Here," she said. The photograph was blurry, and obviously one taken by mistake. There were no people in the picture. A disembodied arm jutted into one side but behind that all you could see was a blurry, sunny distance, with dark shapes in the distance. Elif pointed to one of the tiny dark peaks. "That's where my mother came from," she told him. "People used to say she was naughty too." She paused. "The old women told me that when my mother first came to the village, she was already carrying me in her belly but no one knew at first. She wouldn't tell them who the father was, and some people said I had no father, that my mother was a witch and got me from the devil. They didn't say that to my face. Not the grown-ups anyway.

"I used to ask my mother if I could have a father like most of the other children, and she said I already had one, but that he stayed out all night instead of coming home to her, and once, when he had done this three nights in a row, when the sun came up he turned into a cockerel. She said there was nothing she could do, so she left him there on one of the farms, and came down to our village on the plains."

"My dad says my mummy went away because of cancer."

"Yes," Elif said. "I know." And she kissed Memet on the cheek.

That was the last time he saw her. She had bundled the photographs back into her little suitcase, given Memet a round red boiled sweet to take away with him, and told him to thank his grandmother for the talisman. About a week later, when he came home from school, he saw his grandmother coming out of Elif's block.

"Have you been to see Elif?" he asked her, anxious that he had missed the chance of a visit.

"No Memet, she's not here anymore," his grandmother said.

He stopped in front of her. "Where is she?" he asked.

"Come inside for tea, child," his grandmother said, and took him by the hand.

Instead, Memet heard from others on the estate what had happened, or at least, their versions of it. The baby had decided to come early. Elif had been screaming from inside her flat for hours before one of the neighbours decided to call the police. When they arrived, they had to break down the door, and immediately called an ambulance. Accounts varied as to what was actually delivered. The more sedate versions were that the baby was stillborn, but wilder imaginations postulated everything from the birth of a two-headed boy to a goat. "What is wrong with these people?" Memet Ali's father would say. "Why do they believe such nonsense?" Whatever Elif had given birth to, it hadn't survived. People felt sorry for her, but not that much. *They found out she wasn't meant to be here, of course – I could have told them that a year ago – So what's going to happen to the flat? – What's going to happen to her? – They've sent her home. Wish I could have my plane ticket bought for me. I could do with a bit of proper sunshine.*

For several weeks, Memet would take a short detour after school to walk up to her flat. The door and windows had been boarded over with pale chipboard. Memet would stare at the cheap wood for a few minutes and then go home for tea. Then one day, there was a proper front door again. Memet knocked but no-one answered. When he got home, he asked his grandmother, "What happened to the baby?"

"What baby?" she asked, lighting the oven.

"Elif's baby."

She put in a baking tray. "It died," she said.

"Was it my brother?" Memet asked.

His grandmother stood up. "What makes you say that?"

"I don't know. I just thought it would be nice to have a brother. Or a sister."

Memet's grandmother eyed him carefully. "This will be a while cooking. Why don't you go out and play? You shouldn't be with grown-ups all the time."

Memet went slowly down the stairs and out into the courtyard. A girl from his school was skipping rope by herself.

"Hello," she said.

"Hello," Memet said. "I've got a brother."

"No you haven't," she said.

"I have too."

She stopped skipping. "Then how come I've never seen him."

"He doesn't live here. He lives on a farm."

"Is he a farmer?"

"No, he's a cockerel."

"You can't have a cockerel for a brother," she said.

"Well I have. And Elif's father was a cockerel too."

The girl nodded thoughtfully. She'd heard funny things about Elif.

"I think I heard your brother this morning," she said. "When I woke up I could hear him crowing."

"Yes," Memet said, "that was him."

And then they went to look for bloodstains in the stairwell three blocks down, where a man was supposed to have been stabbed the night before.

Marginalia

Today, in the reading room, you examine a facsimile of a thirteenth-century bestiary, carefully separating each page with your gloved fingers. The original codex comes from a monastery in the North of England. You imagine the naked fingers of damp monks freezing tight around their quills, the chafing of chilblained hands as they create a universe of sun-darkened, heat-hardened mammals, exuberantly scaled reptiles, tropical plants with phalluses for flowers, or unipods – one-legged almost humans – who hop along on one enormous foot, and use it as a canopy against the scorched daylight of an eastern desert.

You love this book. It is your favourite in all the world. In this book the margins at last come to the centre. Monsters and marvels rub along together, verso to recto. In this book the freaks have top billing, while the margins are populated with the mundane: plain monks in ordinary brown cowls, scribing, praying, farming; or drinking ale and coursing, hares and foxes making good their escape in the foliated corners of the page.

And what difference between a monster and a marvel, you want to know as you turn the pages beneath your gloves. You have examined this book many times. You ponder the nature of monstrosity daily.

The book falls open at a picture of a unicorn, its horny head lain down upon the thighs of a virgin. You think, *I have never been kissed.* You touch your lips under the net veil of your hat, but cannot feel them through your gloves.

You first notice him on Monday. He sits next to you at the catalogue terminal, and you watch him fill out the search with book titles you cannot quite read from here. He glances up sideways at you and smiles. You want to smile back. Your hands go up to your hat, adjust your veil slightly, pull it further down in front of your face. You undo the button of your high-neck blouse, then re-button it. You fumble, but not because of the gloves. You are used to doing everything wearing gloves. You watch him get up and take a seat at a desk. You leave the catalogue terminal to sit down at your own seat: you can watch him from here.

You observe how his dark wavy hair falls in front of his eyes while his head is bowed towards the reading material in front of him, so that he has to brush it back with his hands, again and again. You can feel the slick of his hair-oil sliding onto his hands, as if they were your own hands and you had no gloves, instead leaving a trail of dirty fingerprints on the filmy paper of your books. You wonder if he noticed where you sat down. You are afraid he will look up and see you. You are afraid he won't look up.

On Tuesday there is an unfamiliar woman behind the desk. The others are used to you by now, but she stares as you queue to collect your books. You hear her ask another member of staff whether readers are allowed to keep hats and gloves on in the reading room. The librarian follows her gaze, realises she is referring to you, and gives her a lengthy reply that you do not hear. She nods and continues fetching the called-up books. You hope that someone else will serve you, but when you get to the head of the queue she is the one who asks for your desk number. When she speaks, it is clear that the other librarian has explained your situation to her, your special dispensation. She tries to sound casual and friendly, but doesn't. You look at her mouse-coloured hair, her thin taupe lips, her timid forehead. She is plain and mundane like the monks in the margins of your beloved manuscript.

You think, *no-one would notice her if she walked into a room.* You tell her your desk number and she gives you your books. When you turn around, the dark-haired man you met at the catalogue terminal yesterday is behind you. You blush, you feel as red as your suit, and almost drop your books. But he has already stepped up to the counter. You walk back to your desk.

You don't normally take a break for lunch, but at noon on Wednesday when you see the dark-haired man get up and put on his jacket, you decide to get up too and follow him outside. At the door you have to show your clear plastic bag to the security guard so that she can examine the contents inside. Then you are free to walk out into the public area, where you follow him into the self-service canteen. You watch him pick up a tray from a pile, so you do the same.

"Hello," he says.

"Hello," you reply, but it comes out as a croak, because the only other words you have spoken, all week, were to tell the library staff your desk number, and to ask for a travelcard at the newsagents. You clear your throat and pretend you are recovering from a cold.

"Great hat," he tells you. "I love all those old black and white movies."

What luck. He imagines that's why you dress like this, why you wear a hat with a net veil, the gloves that always conceal your hands. You wonder if he might think you affected, as people often do.

"Michael," he says, holding out his hand. You hold out your gloved hand in return. You cannot feel the texture of his fingers or his palm – only their slight pressure on yours – but when you shake hands a shock of static runs between you. You pull back quickly with an embarrassed croak and pick up your tray again. You tell him your name.

"That's a pretty name," he says. "Where's it from?"

It's always your name that gives you away, underneath the hat and the gloves and the clothes, underneath the voice that sounds just like theirs. You tell him its origin and he nods. You notice that his eyes are grey in the light of the canteen. In the reading room they had appeared a dark shade of blue. In either case, they stir you to breathlessness: like the start of a panic attack. You sit down together for lunch, although you only have a cold drink on your tray, in a carton with a straw.

"I don't normally have lunch," you explain.

You raise the straw to your lips, underneath the netting. You know that lunch is a bad idea because he can see that you won't take your hat off, nor your gloves, not even to eat or drink. You watch his face as he realises for the first time that he cannot see any part of you beneath your clothing. He focuses instead on the tray in front of him, on the sandwiches he has chosen, his apple and pot of tea.

He asks about your research and you tell him about the manuscripts, about the margins with their monsters and beasts, and all the fell creatures that have no place other than on the edges of things.

"Monsters?" He smiles. "Like those maps that say 'here be dragons'?"

His own research is on British naval history. You tell him about the maps where the world is a circle divided by a seascape in the form of a cross, with its top limb missing. You explain about the earthly paradise, in the east; you explain that the closer to paradise, the more densely populated with monsters.

"Britain," you tell him "appears on such maps as a strange cold island in the far west, as far away from paradise as can be imagined; a little thing populated by ghosts, right on the edge of the world."

This makes him smile too, but as you would to the frayed

old man on your bus who sings to himself.

When you get home that night you don't immediately take off your hat and gloves but you do unbutton your coat. You feel hot. It's not just the contrast with the cold night outside. You can feel the heat rising through your body, underneath your clothes, underneath your hair and skin. You peer into the dim mirror in the bathroom, the only mirror in your flat, and hold your gloved hands up to the sides of your face beneath the netting of the 'forties-style hat. Only shadows can be seen beneath the veil, the fact that you have eyes and a mouth. You turn, first one way, then the other. Beneath the stylized clothing you look normal. *This is all he sees*, you say to yourself. And then you call his name out loud into the flat: *Michael*. But the empty echo makes you shiver, despite the flush you can feel working its way up your spine. You cover over the mirror with a towel and undress with your eyes closed.

On Thursday you make notes on a facsimile of a fourteenth-century travelogue. On one leaf is a line drawing, with a scrolled caption at the bottom that reads, when translated into English, as 'Community of Monsters'. Once there existed an accompanying text that revealed the nature of their monstrosity but that page is now missing – torn out or burnt. You examine the surviving picture closely, as you always do, trying to work out why these particular creatures were deemed monstrous. They look human to you, these half-dozen naked men and women living in caves in a desert oasis, hunting, cooking. Gentle brushstrokes across their skin indicate hair, a bristly down that covers their entire bodies. Are they monsters because of their wild-pig hairiness? Or because they refuse to cover it up? You imagine them dressed in the clothes of the people around you in the reading room, and as you look around you see Michael sitting in a far corner, head bent low, hands brushing away the curling hair from his forehead. You've never seen him sit so far back before. You wonder if he is avoiding you.

On Friday he fails to see you behind him in the queue for the counter. The new librarian is serving again.

"Good morning Susan," you hear him say.

"Hello Mike," she replies. *Mike?*

Susan goes to fetch his books. She takes her time handing them over. You notice that their fingers touch. She sees you in the queue and blushes. Michael turns in the direction of her blush. You watch him take in your costume. He nods a half-smiled good morning to you, glances back to Susan, and takes his books.

Susan puts on her false, bright smile and asks for your desk number, slowly and loudly as if you might have difficulty understanding. You don't answer at first, just stand there staring at her. Her hair is the colour of dishwater after you have spilled cold coffee in the sink. Her eyes are the colour of unwashed beer bottles held up to the light. Her lips are thin as the tapered ends of chopsticks. You want to slap her in the face, hard. You want to set a stopwatch on how long it would take the bright red mark of your gloveprint to fade. Instead you give her your desk number. She gives you your books.

But she is nervous; her gaze has faltered under your gaze and her hands grow sweaty. The books fall. You look down at them, see where they have fallen to your feet, see your shoes that are so thick with shine and polish that you could, if you wished, lift your veil and look at your distorted image in their curved reflection.

"I'm so sorry," Susan wails.

You don't say anything, but bend to retrieve the disarrayed volumes. And somehow you become unbalanced as you bend down. You tumble sideways. You become disheveled. A reader behind you – you don't know whether it's a man or a woman – reaches out a hand to steady you, but you push them away. Susan gasps. You quickly adjust your hat, your veil, but it's too late. She has already seen your face.

"Oh my god," she says.

"Sssshhh," hushes one of the other librarians, mortified at Susan's lapse of tact. Still, Susan stares at your veiled hat in horror, at your gloves, at your high-button blouse. Other staff and readers gather at both sides of the counter and pretend not to peer at you.

"But there's nothing wrong with her," says Susan.

You think, *she sounds genuinely disturbed.*

"There's nothing wrong with her."

"What?" asks Susan's colleague. And like her, he has only enough words to repeat himself: "What?"

You sense them watching you as you straighten up with the books, walk back to your desk and quietly get on with your research. Whenever you look up, in whatever direction, heads slide away, as if they had been turned to you only a moment before. Only later do you remember Michael. You look up from your books. You look up, but you cannot see him anywhere.

You turn the pages of your favourite bestiary, and trace a gloved index finger around the monstrous outlines centre-paged, marveling at the variety of deformity. Your finger follows the curve of the Blemeye, a headless creature that wears its face on its torso. The Blemeye holds up a club and brandishes it at a Cyclops. In turn the one-eyed giant holds in its expansive hand a squint-eyed Pygmy wielding a bow and arrow. Blemeye, Cyclops and Pygmy stare out at you from the manuscript. Below these creatures, the unknown scribe has inked-in the figure of a girl, ordinary and plain, squeezed tight into the margin. She sits with her face half-hidden as she reads a tiny book, right off the edge of the text.

Surf Scoter

Vernon was named after the football pools because he was conceived on the day his dad won fifty quid on the no-score draws. It was the last piece of good luck Vernon's dad had. Walking home from the pub two weeks after the celebrations were over, he slipped in a puddle and cracked his head on the edge of a jutting-out square of pavement. Blood seeped into the puddle with the rain and lapped at the feet of a man and a dog out for a late night walk.

Vernon's mother, Cathy, cursed her dead boyfriend and pursed her lips tight with contempt and worry. She was forced to open them eight and a half months later, screaming with labour pains. It was Cathy who chose the name Vernon, in memory of the ill-fated pools win; an old-man's name that he was sure to get tormented about at school. Cathy hoped that its connotations of tedium and mediocrity would save him from the reckless path of his late father.

Vernon, on the other hand, always thought of himself as a love child.

"What was my dad like?" he would ask, endlessly, despite the tight-lipped warnings of his mother's face. Mostly, Cathy wouldn't answer. When she did, it was in language Vernon wasn't allowed to use himself.

Once, Cathy nursed a black eye after a fight with a blonde

woman who lived three streets away and who had knocked on their door one teatime. Vernon had been eating toast in the kitchen and didn't take any notice of their conversation until he heard the two women screaming curses at each other. He ran into the corridor clutching his toast, dropping crumbs on the lino. Through the open door Vernon saw his mum and the blonde woman tearing at each other's hair, swearing and punching. A couple of the neighbouring husbands managed to separate them.

One of the women next door winked at Vernon, who was eight years old.

"And do you take after your da, with his eye for the birds?"

Vernon didn't know what to say, so just stood there and took a bite out of his toast.

"Aye, I'll bet you do," she said. "Men, you're all the bloody same, from eight years old to eighty."

By this time Cathy had shaken off the men holding her back and was storming back up to the house.

"Get inside Vernon!"

Vernon ran back to the kitchen and pondered the information he had just received about his dad's inclination for birds, while his mum bathed her cuts and held a packet of frozen peas to her eye. Venon saw that they were called 'Birds Eye' and from then on declared that peas were his favourite food, even though he disliked the colour green.

At the age of ten, Vernon knew the names of all the sea

birds that flocked into Gaunt each summer. At twelve, he could identify all the sea birds along the eastern coast. By the time he was fourteen, he knew all the birds of Britain. His mum approved.

"He's a quiet lad," she'd say to the woman who sold newspapers at the corner shop. "Only cares about his birds, and listening to his music."

"It's the quiet ones you've got to watch out for," intoned the newspaper lady on autopilot.

"Not my Vernon," Cathy would shake her head. "Not my boy."

And she'd pay for her cigarettes and newspaper and walk home puffing like an old seagull. Cathy knew Vernon would never leave her.

Now he was seventeen, with an inordinate fondness for waterfowl. His mum had a set of three ornamental ducks nailed to the wall of the sitting room, flying over the television in formation. Vernon had always found this strange, flying but not going anywhere. He started to wish that his mum's flying ducks would disappear, that one morning he would come down for breakfast and find that they had migrated. He wondered what his mum's reaction would be. Not good, he thought. Cathy didn't much like the thought of losing anything, whether an umbrella on the bus, a penny from her purse, or an argument. Everything had to be kept close and under control, including, Vernon knew, himself.

Vernon got a job at the local record store. It was so small that only one other person worked there apart from Vernon, and that was the owner, Mr Peterson. Cathy hadn't wanted Vernon to get a job at first, but had to concede they needed the money. Her own job up at the hotel on the seafront was seasonal, "like the birds" Vernon had explained to Mr Peterson.

One day, after Vernon had been working in the shop for a couple of months, Mr Peterson said all casual-like, "I knew your dad, you know."

Vernon felt himself grow hot.

"Aye," the man continued, "Big Ramones fan, your dad." This was news indeed.

"The Ramones?" Vernon asked, incredulously. His mum only listened to female crooners with big voices. Vernon had to listen to his own music with headphones on so as not to disturb his mum. He usually took his music player out with him when he was watching the birds on the seafront; often he went out to see the birds just to get away from the Titanic soundtrack. His mum was a big fan of Celine Dion and 'My Heart Will Go On'.

"What about The Clash?" asked Vernon, who had an unappeased love for 70s British punk.

"Oh aye, your dad liked all them bands. But The Ramones were his favourite. Always wanted to go to the States himself.

We even thought about going together, you know, mebbes start a band ourselves. San Francisco way, near the coast still, but with a chance of sunshine. Not like this ball-freezing dump."

Vernon absorbed this new, unexpected information. He borrowed some Ramones CDs off Mr Peterson. Later in the week he went to the library to use the computers. He googled 'American Punk' and 'San Francisco Birds'. Within a few months he knew the names of all the birds that migrated to the San Francisco Bay estuary. Alongside this, he found out everything he could about the punk scene there, at least, everything that could be gleaned from the web or from music magazines. Vernon had a gift for focus and details.

Cathy was getting worried. "You call that rubbish music?" she sneered, when Mr Peterson's 'Rocket to Russia' fell out of his rucksack. But the sneer came out more whiny than she intended and Vernon winced.

"You never told me Mr Peterson knew my dad," he challenged.

Cathy blanched. "Told you that, did he?" she asked. "I might've known he'd have not kept his mouth shut."

"Dad didn't think The Ramones were rubbish," Vernon said.

"Aye, well, your dad didn't think full stop. But you're not like him son, believe me."

"Well, mebbes I am, more than you think," Vernon replied.

His voice was a bit shaky. He wasn't used to answering back to his mum, and she wasn't used to hearing it.

"Where's me tabs?" she asked, pretending not to have heard him. He found her cigarettes and threw them over to her. He went up to his room, put down his rucksack and got his binoculars out instead.

"Going out to see the birds, pet?" Cathy asked when she saw him downstairs. An attempt at reconciliation. Vernon grunted a nod and quickly went out before she could say anything else.

Without telling his mum, Vernon opened a postal saving account with a building society in Newcastle. He used the address of the record store so she wouldn't find out. Within a year, he'd saved enough for a cheap plane ticket to the States and some money to get by for a week or so. After that, he'd have to find work, cash in hand, because he wouldn't have a green card. Vernon also applied for a passport, his first, asking his boss to countersign the unflattering photo-booth pictures. He knew Mr Peterson wouldn't tell anyone.

"Good for you lad," Mr Peterson said, when Vernon told him about wanting a passport. "It's good for a man to stretch his legs."

At home, arguments were flaring up over the smallest things. Vernon was extremely tidy, especially in contrast to Cathy, and was often clearing up her belongings.

"Where's my lipstick?" she'd yell, or, "What happened to

that letter from the leccy?" Vernon would point to where he'd carefully placed them. Cathy would flip.

"Just leave my stuff alone can't you? What's wrong with you?"

Vernon didn't care that Cathy was no longer proud of how neat he was, telling all the neighbours what a good son she had. He knew she was starting to get unsettled by his behaviour. Vernon had always been a quiet lad, but these days he could hardly bear to talk to his mum at all.

On the day his plane tickets arrived, Vernon packed up some belongings and folded them into his rucksack. It bulged in odd directions and jutted into his back when he lifted it up. He pored over the details of his journey. He had to catch a train to London via Newcastle and then travel on the Underground to connect to Heathrow airport. He decided to catch the very first train out of Gaunt, which would be well before his mum had woken up. Vernon didn't go to sleep that night, he sat on his bed fully clothed, listening to The Ramones through his headphones. An hour or so before dawn he put on his jacket, picked up his rucksack and crept downstairs. His mum's bedroom door was open and he could hear her snoring. Downstairs he paused. It was strange, he had to admit, leaving like this. He'd never been abroad before, he'd not even been out of Gaunt much, except to Newcastle of course; and once he'd been to Edinburgh on a school trip. Maybe it wasn't such a good idea. His mum would be heartbroken and she wasn't that bad, considering.

As he hesitated in the darkness a glint caught his eye from the sitting room. He walked in and saw the three ornamental flying ducks, outlined in the dark room by the light from the streetlamp. On impulse, Vernon went over to the wall and pulled them off, one by one. They left behind clean un-nicotine-stained duck-shaped patches on the wallpaper. Holding the ducks in the crook of one arm, he let himself out of the house quietly and strolled out into the pre-dawn morning. Instead of walking directly to the train station, he went via the cliff and the sea front. Most people wouldn't be able to see the various birds nesting in the cliff-face but Vernon knew where to look. He stood there on the beach, looking up at the sleeping birds in their nests for about half an hour. He grew cold. Then he shook himself, and walked back up to the road and to the station.

*

There was a knock on Cathy's door. Cathy opened it to find a postman - not her usual one - standing on the doorstep with a large parcel, wrapped up in brown paper.

"Got a whopper here for you, pet," he said.

"I can't carry that," she protested.

"Eh, no worries, it's big but it's light," he said, handing it over. And it was.

"Ta," said Cathy and shut the door.

She took the parcel into the living room. It was huge, almost half the size of the coffee table. Cathy squinted at the stamps. Puerto Rico. She shrugged, and started to peel off the brown paper. Underneath was more brown paper, with more stamps - this time from Costa Rica. More peeling off, more brown paper, more stamps: Buenos Aires, Tokyo, Moscow, Prague, Sydney, Manila, Phnom Penh. The parcel unravelled into a smaller and smaller bundle, while the sitting room floor became strewn with more and more torn and crumpled fragments of brown parcel paper, until Cathy was down to what must surely be the last sheet. Beneath her fingers she could feel something hard inside. She could hear and feel edges moving against each other, as if maybe whatever was swaddled inside was broken, or perhaps was made of different parts.

Cathy ripped open the last piece of brown paper. Inside, gleaming up at her, were her three ornamental ducks, well-travelled and gloriously world-weary, to hang back up on the wall.

Maganda

Inang said, "Not every creature wearing human skin is a human being."

Everyone called her Inang, which means 'mother', although in fact she was my grandmother. The Saturday morning before my ninth birthday she grasped my hand as we walked through the marshes, past the reservoirs and down Coppermill Lane to the market, where she was going to buy me a dress.

"What do you mean, Inang?" I had prompted, thinking she was about to tell me another story.

But instead of a story, Inang started to sing in a low voice to herself, one of those songs in her language that I couldn't understand, and so I quickly lost interest, caught up in a fantasy of the new dress. With covetous imagination, I had a vision of a little sailor outfit, with a blue-trimmed collar that would flap in a square at the back and tie in a neat little bow at the front, and frilly ankle socks, and burnished red shoes that had a strap across the front like a tap dancer's shoes.

Inang would not be able to afford anything like that. She gazed down and asked if there was something I wanted in particular.

"No, Inang," I said. But then, because I was still an eight-year-old girl after all, added, "Something pretty."

Inang smiled and patted my hand.

"Yes, of course. Something pretty, for my pretty girl."

Inang was the only one who ever called me that. Every morning in the bathroom, Mum would hold my head in her hands and grip the sides of my face with a pinched movement of her thumb and index finger. She twisted my head from side to side over the sink, as if to examine better all defects from various angles. My ears hummed, while my head was held face down under the cold water. Mum would sing a strangled parody of an old song: your face will never be your fortune.

That Saturday, Inang bought me a red cotton dress from the market, chosen from an overstuffed plastic rack that had a yellow cardboard starburst with 'under £5' scrawled on in a thick black marker-pen. The dress had short puffed sleeves, a frilled edge at the hem and a low square neck with a shirred bodice. It was the prettiest dress I ever owned, before I grew old enough to make money and choose my own clothes. Mum wasn't one to dress me like a doll. Instead I would wear the cast-offs of various cousins, or drab acrylic polo-neck pullovers in bottle green, beige or navy that ribbed tight around my flat chest and wrists. Inconspicuous colours. Camouflage. Inang would not have wanted me to hide or disguise myself, but a few weeks after my ninth birthday she died. I was not allowed to go to the funeral, but I still had to wear black.

Twenty-one years later there is no one left with the power

to forbid me to attend this funeral and I do so want to watch my mother's casket slide into the bleak gleam of the crematorium fire. I still have to wait; yes, I do. This being my mother, the whole process of disposing of the corpse is an anfractuous route of vigil, service, fire, wake. I am wearing a scarlet dress for the occasion. It makes the old women's heads turn in the pews and with one voice, like an amen, they tut-tut-tut as I clatter down the aisle in my four-inch-heeled courts the colour of the Devil.

"Sus-mary-osep!" an old woman blasphemes in a loud whisper, and her turquoise rosary beads fall to her feet.

"No respect, naman!" another crone exclaims in delighted agreement.

Once I reach my seat in the front pew, I turn my head to acknowledge the congregation, smile at the crones in the pews behind me. Their shudder is a Mexican wave that runs through the church, across the aisle.

I have always liked Ecclesiastes. The words from the pulpit drift over our heads and I nod in agreement: "A time to weep, and a time to laugh. A time to mourn, and a time to dance." I turn around once again to face the blaspheming old women. Their heads immediately slip away from mine to face the priest. I turn back and can almost see their faces swivel again towards me, through the back of my head.

The priest reads from Revelation 22: "Nothing accursed will be found there any more … They will look upon his face, and his name will be on their foreheads."

Like the mark of Cain, but of course I don't say that out loud, merely stifle a giggle, holding up my freshly laundered handkerchief to my mouth like a widow at a murder trial.

More words at the crematorium. How tiresome ritual can be. I would have liked to choose the music myself, something in the vein of 'Disco Inferno', with its exhortation to combust. But mum wanted Diana Ross and made her own arrangements with her cronies, so 'Disco Inferno' will have to wait for my own passing beyond the vale. Mum's coffin passes through the red velvet curtain to the sounds of 'Do You Know Where You're Going To?', and I need to raise my handkerchief to my face once more. One of the crones mistakes my mirth for grief and touches me compassionately on my forearm. I stiffen at the infraction and she pulls away.

"You are coming to the wake?" she says to me afterwards, the statement masquerading as a question.

"In a while," I reply. "I need some time alone first."

Her wrinkled lips purse, so that her slack aged mouth looks like a lunar crater filled in with pink lipstick, but she nods. I exit into a waiting taxi.

I have already moved into the family home my mother left, an ex-council flat on the fourth floor of Hrothgar House, on the Kingsmead Estate in Clapton, between Homerton High Street and Daubeney Road. All the houses look the same: closed stairwells with new entryphones, each flat refurbished with identical brown varnished doors, red paint around the doors and windows of each floor, and new plastic white window-frames like Lego sections. From the balcony I can see Hackney Marshes in the near distance, with its football pitches and spiny shadows. When I was a child, everyone at school believed there was a bear on the marshes. Mum believed it too.

"Don't go there alone," she'd tell me. "The bear might get you."

Then she'd pause.

"Although who knows?" she'd say. "Maybe you're safe. Maybe the bear will be frightened of you and run away." And she'd pinch my face, hard and laugh.

"Dios Ko! What an ugly child."

It was God's curse. Whether on her or on me was never made clear.

We are all born in sin.

On Saturday mornings or Sunday afternoons Inang would take my hand, and we'd go to the marshes and we'd walk and walk and walk. I was afraid of the bear, but Inang would shush me, and wipe the sweated fringe of hair from my forehead, tuck it behind my ears.

"There's no bear here. And even if there was, it's not the creatures who wear their fur on the outside that should scare you." Her bony fingers gently brushed the thick down on my face.

Sometimes we would watch the football. Local boys mostly, some I recognized from school, too busy moving their feet around the small pitches and shouting to each other to call out names to me. Goalposts massed together on the marshes like white turbines in a wind farm. Mothers, stood at the sides to guard jackets and bags, would not look at me. Or they would look at me, without caring that I could see them looking at me. And sometimes a mother would look at me and smile, and that was worst of all.

"Say hello," Inang would prompt.

And I'd say hello and wave. That should have been the woman's cue to say, "What an adorable child," or "What a lovely girl." Occasionally, one of them was able to manage a "How sweet" before turning back to the football. Sweet. Like a kitten or a poodle. At such times I wanted the bear to finally make its appearance, grim and greedy, and claim me for its own. But Inang would stroke my head, or hold my hand, and I would feel calm again and the mist that gathered in front of my eyes would clear.

On the days when there was no football or it was too cold to stay still, or on the days when there were too many people around who might look and point and cry out, on those days we would walk. Along the river path beside the marshes, over a bridge and back again, onto Walthamstow Marshes and the swans on the River Lea. A change from the grey pigeons that gathered on the estate and elsewhere, that painted the ground and crumbling brick walls off-white with their never-ending droppings. I would run ahead and brush my matted fingers over cow parsley and dock leaves. Inang would pick nettles sometimes and boil them up at home to brew a foul-tasting tea.

As we walked, Inang would tell me stories. From the islands, she said. Over seven thousand of them and each one different. Some had mountains and stretched so far you couldn't tell you were surrounded by ocean. Others had fields of rice, older than Jesus and cut into the hills like temples. On some islands, there were more turtles than people and at night the women would grow flippers and swim out into the sea with a shell on their back. On the islands, the women were always turning into something else.

"Like mermaids?" I'd ask. Mermaids were respectable. We read about them in stories at school.

"Pah." Inang made a sound with her lips to dismiss the mermaids.

"Naked women," she said, with her mouth turned down, "who sing for fishing folk, or else cut off their tongues for the love of a man. No child," she'd say, "that's not our women." And she would tell me stories of women who drank the blood of their enemies. Manananggals, women who can separate their body from their legs, to fly up into other people's houses at night on the wings of a bat. An aswang, who has the ability to transform into a pig, a dog or a bird, and will steal a dead body and replace it with a wooden carving. Tikbalang a half-human, half-four-footed creature who leads travellers astray by mimicking the voice or appearance of a close relative and calling to the travellers to follow them, into the woods or into the cavernous depths of mountains.

"To protect yourself," Inang said, "when you travel, you must walk with your clothes worn inside out, so they do not recognize you."

"Ay nako, Inang!" Mum said, irritated, when I had explained to her why I had come home from school with my anorak turned inside out to show the orange lining. "Stop filling her head with such nonsense." And she pinched me, hard, on the fatty part of my left thigh. It doesn't matter about bruises, because you can't see them beneath the hair.

The wake is being held in a community hall in Manor Park, near the cemetery. Anyone who dies with an East London postcode ends up in this cemetery, loosely bordered by Ilford, Stratford, East Ham and Wanstead, that dead gash of land between London and Essex. I hadn't organized the hall. Like the funeral, this has been taken care of by Mum's cronies. I'm not certain 'wake' is the right term. When I get to the hall, the gathering seems more like an extended karaoke session fed with pancit noodles and chicken adobo, lots and lots of Coca-Cola and black coffee, and tuba, a strong spirit wine made from coconut trees that would have been sweet only on the day it was tapped from the tree. In the time it has taken to get to England the tuba has soured into bitterness.

All the songs being sung are either Diana Ross covers or numbers from musicals. When I arrive, the old woman who had dropped her rosary beads in church is doing a belting rendition of 'Somewhere over the Rainbow'. She even looks a little like Judy Garland as Dorothy, dark hair tied in plaits and slightly overweight, but with a lot more wrinkles and much darker skin. Judy Garland as shrivelled walnut.

Compassionate crone pops up at my elbow. She's that short.

"Eh, Maganda, where have you been?"

"I wanted to change into something more comfortable," I tell her.

She looks at me. I am still wearing my scarlet dress.

I point to my feet. She looks down. I have swapped my high-heeled court shoes for a pair of eight-hole patent cherry-red Doc Martens boots. Just in case I want to go for a walk.

Her pink-lipsticked lips purse again, like they did in the church. I'm guessing it's a favourite expression of hers.

"Why don't I get you some tuba?" I ask her.

"I'm not drinking any alcohol until I've been up for my first song."

I don't want to ask, but can't help myself.

"What are you going to sing?"

"A Whole New World," she says.

From the Disney version of *Aladdin*.

"It's a Pinoy classic," she says.

It really isn't.

I ask if I can go up next. I'm warming to the idea of singing karaoke at my mother's wake. A time to dance. A time to laugh.

Compassionate crone immediately looks suspicious.

"What do you want to sing?" she asks me.

"Oh, I don't know," I lie. "A standard from *The Wizard of Oz*, perhaps."

She clicks her tongue, making a noise like a gecko.

"We don't have 'The Wicked Witch is Dead'," she tells me.

Am I really so transparent? Or is the gecko a mind-reader?

The rosary-dropping Judy Garland crone is coming to the end of her second number – 'Get Happy'– and everyone applauds. Another old woman takes to the stage, this time a shrivelled bag of bones doing a passable impersonation of Doris Day crossed with Yoda the Jedi. The hall is full of old Filipino women, women who you never see anywhere except at funerals and under the dryers at the hairdresser's. There are no men here. I can't even begin to care why that might be.

I decide to leave when Doris-Yoda starts singing 'Once I Had A Secret Love' from *Calamity Jane*. All my life I'd thought it would be fun to dance on my mother's grave. But that really only works when everyone else is weeping. I had underestimated the essentially cheerful nature of Tagalog ritual.

Compassionate crone grabs my arm.

"Where are you going?"

"No pancit is worth this," I tell her, "no matter how well cooked."

And I stomp out in my cherry-red boots. The crone looks worried and calls out to me, but I start to run and can't hear what she is saying. I carry on running until I get to the Romford Road. Then I slow down and walk for about five minutes, until there's a cab office ahead of me, tucked between a Chinese takeaway and a newsagent that is now closed for the night. Above, Venus is low on the horizon, just starting to rise over the rooftops.

There are sweat stains on my scarlet dress from the running and they've seeped into the thin jacket I've worn over it, so there's no disguising them. So much for glamour. It's the hair, of course. So efficient at trapping body heat.

There's a woman with electric-blue eyeshadow behind the window of the cab office and she looks up, startled. Ah, yes. Years of painful electrolysis on my face and hands have shaved me into some semblance of a woman, but I'm still shaggier than Bigfoot under a full moon. I smile, and hope the cab controller will overlook the sweat-stained dress and Doc Martens and overhanging eyebrows.

"Can I help you love?"

"Cab to Homerton please," I say casually. As if I've just popped in from the takeaway next door. As if I've not just run away from a karaoke keening in honour of my dead mother, organized by a coven with a taste for musicals and Benedictine kitsch.

The bright-blue eyelids flicker but the controller's voice, to her credit, is steady.

"Fifteen minutes." And she gestures to a plastic padded chair.

I sit down and flick through an ancient copy of *Hello!* Magazine.

"Thank you," I tell her. I'm still sweating.

The cab driver takes us the wrong way, and then, as we approach from an unnecessary direction, he refuses to go any further when he spots the old Hackney Hospital looming up in front of us on Homerton High Street. It's an odd building, I admit, especially with that full moon rising up behind the Victorian prison-workhouse silhouette of the lunatic block, but really, you can take superstition too far.

"But it's just another minute to Kingsmead," I say.

"No."

We haggle and he takes two quid off the fare. Then I get out of the car. The driver does a perfect, illegal U-turn and zooms off in the wrong direction.

The High Street is dead. I walk down Marsh Hill and Homerton Road and turn off into the estate. Hrothgar House is over on the other side, by Clapton Park, past Ironside, Offa's Mead, Lindisfarne and Jarrow Way. I walk by various houses: Alfred, Aethelred, Aethelstan. It should only take me a few minutes to walk through Kingsmead to get back home to Hrothgar House. But, unaccountably, I take a wrong turn and here I am, outside Aethelred House again. And I didn't even drink the tuba.

There's a noise of bees swarming which makes no sense until I work out it's the wind in the guttering above me. I hadn't noticed the breeze was up when I got out of the cab, but I am definitely feeling it now. My back and under my arms dry cold where the wet stains are, and the sharp air that whips the fringe over my eyes makes my forehead feel like I've eaten an ice cream too fast. It's the sweat, of course: so efficient at lowering body temperature. My body. It all just works so damn perfect.

Unlike my brain, which is having difficulty focusing on basic compass directions. I'm walking through the estate in a straight line, except it can't be, because I'm back in front of Aethelred House and the bees are buzzing in the drainpipes again.

The estate looks different. Pre-refurbishment, more like how I remember it as a child, each section four storeys of brown brick and balcony, piss-stained open-access stairwells and overflowing oversized metal bins. Virtually every window and front door is fenced over with sinuous black metal railings, the window bars curving out like goldfish bags swollen with water. And then I hear the whisper behind me. I turn around but there's no one there. It's just the wind.

"Maganda." Mum's voice. Mum's idea of a joke: my name means beautiful. The name of the first woman in Filipino creation, falling into the world from out of one half of a split bamboo stalk. I prefer to tell people my name is Maggie. Less alien. At the hospital they call me Shaggy Maggie.

"Maganda." The second voice sounds like Inang's, whispery with age but sure and certain, exactly the way I imagine that I remember it.

I believe in the truth of all stories, but that doesn't mean I have to believe they're really true. I don't believe in these voices. But still, I turn around to see where they're coming from. Even though I know it's the wind. I turn back around, in time to see a movement in front of me, a flash of shadow, dark in the darkness, rounding the corner of Aethelred House, like a big cat or a small wolf. Someone's pet out for a late-night dump, I decide, certain that I'm not going to follow it for any reason. Instead I walk in a straight line, heading for Hrothgar House. I don't end up at Hrothgar House, and I don't end up back at Aethelred House either. Inexplicably, unreasonably, against all narrative causality, I am standing on the marshes, like I've taken one giant stride over Kingsmead and the River Lea in my big red boots, and now there's nothing ahead of me but goalposts.

And in case you're wondering – this isn't a dream.

She's here, the likeness of my grandmother, hand up

against a goalpost to steady herself, her other hand unseen behind the back of the likeness of my mother. Close to, their features lose focus, Seurat dots that only make sense from a distance or a photograph taken with a myopic lens. And they're standing too close to each other. So close you could believe their bodies are joined up, like a person with four legs.

Not every creature wearing human skin is a human being.

I pick up my feet to run away, but my boots squelch and pop in the marsh as mud sucks up to fill the new space. The two heads swivel soundlessly round on a stock-still torso until they face me.

"Maganda," they call out, in unison, and a smile spreads over the two faces, wide, and then wider, too, too wide, until there is nothing but a single giant maw collapsing the two shapes, gaping across the breadth of the goal line. Its breath is cold and rank, with the stagnant smell of standing water and marshland. Crane flies and clouds of midges buzz from out of the enormous jaw and marsh water drips down the sides like drool.

It knows my name.

This isn't a dream.

But the shape of my name in the creature's mouth is decaying, along with its semblance of humanity, into one long howl of unrecognizable sound. Its pitch rises, over my head, above the goalposts, higher than the last remaining tower block in Clapton Park. All the dogs on the Kingsmead

Estate start to bark. They howl in sympathy. The creature's cry rises still further until the frequency is so high I cannot hear it and my face aches on both sides, from my ears to my jaws and inside my teeth, down the sides of my shaven neck. A colony of bats, wings fluttering faster than swifts, zooms into the clouds of insects that are pouring out of the marsh-mouth. An owl swoops down low and rises back up with a small rodent clutched between its claws. The owl's feathers brush my face and I glimpse its victim, squirming. And do I remain statue-still during this howl? I do not. I squirm and curl like a question mark and hold my hands over my ears and hold my face and cross my arms over my body like a shield.

My jaws ache.

This is where I should wake up and find out, like Dorothy, that it's all a dream. Or suddenly notice that the bright object in the sky I thought was Venus appears to be getting brighter and larger and is, in fact, an asteroid about to impact. Some kind of deus ex machina. I am so beyond prayer in this lifetime, but right now my head hurts, my scarlet dress is covered in sweat, midges and marshland, and I am clicking my cherry-red boots like hell for home.

And then the scream stops.

When the scream stops, all the sounds it had been blocking out seep back: the whine of biting insects; the rattle of goalposts in the wind; the hum of night traffic on Homerton Road; a freight train from Walthamstow, rumbling across the tracks over the marshes on its way to Liverpool

Street; a jumbo jet descending on its flight path to Heathrow. Before me stands a creature, four-footed and knock-kneed in its alien landscape, slack jaw dripping saliva like teardrops.

To protect yourself, you must wear your clothes inside out so they do not recognize you. I take off my jacket. I even take off my dress, tugging it over my head. The wind ruffles my fur like stripes of grass stubble bending in a field. I turn the dress inside out, pull the sleeves of the jacket through the armholes and reclothe myself.

This displaced creature, with its hungry, homesick cry, closes its jaw and turns tail. It scampers off, across the marshes. I follow it with my eyes as far as I can in the dark. At a distance, I see it pause suddenly in front of a darker patch of movement in the night, something that causes it to veer off sharply in another direction. Exit, pursued by a bear.

All stories are true, somewhere.

I trudge across the marshes to the bridge that crosses over the River Lea to Daubeney Road. There are no giant strides. Instead I walk the unlit short-cut through Clapton Park back to Kingsmead and Hrothgar House. There's a snuffling animal, part bulldog, part not-even-the-mother-knows-what, left out for the night by its owner and burying a decomposing owl in the bushes next to the path. The dog pads over to me and nuzzles my hand. I pet it for a while and it follows me back to the estate.

This time, I find my way home.

Freak Show

Every summer, when the Hoppings comes to the moor, I say, "let's go look at the freak show." Every summer, Tommy refuses.

"You must be joking," he says. "It's so 19th century," which of course it is, in an Elephant Man kind of way. I like that, but Tommy thinks it's morbid.

Tommy goes strictly for the white-knuckle rides. Magic Mouse: the biggest mobile roller coaster in Europe. ("Tame, very tame," Tommy says.) The rush of the Big Ben tower. The reverse bungee-jump, that swings you upward using what looks like an oversized catapault (£10 a go).

Whereas I get sick on fairground rides. Of course. I'd like to go on the children's rides: gently spinning teacups or the carousel. But I'm way *way* beyond the permitted weight. I don't mind the big wheel, except I always forget how high the Hoppings' Big Wheel actually is, until I'm already going up and it's too late to change my mind.

We went on it last year. Tommy kept shifting his weight to force our capsule into a spin, and laughed as I gripped the bars around our seats, practically throwing myself to the floor. He stood up and leant over the side, dangerously.

"Look at me," he laughed. "Look at me." That's Tommy. Beautiful, brainy, bastard Tommy. He stopped laughing, though, when I vomited over his vintage *Screeching Weasel* t-shirt.

There are a score of women in caravans, each claiming to be genuine Romany Gypsies with the gift of foresight. Some claim to have told the fortunes of Bet Lynch, Ken Barlow, Pauline Fowler. No one thinks to say, but those people are fictions, they don't exist in real life. Tired blonde women with lined faces queue like Soviet-bloc housewives for a better future (£5 for palms, £15 for tarot), carrying plastic bags, twisting wedding rings or fiddling with gold rope chains, or huge hoop earrings; their blistered, sockless feet in trainers, or kitten heels sinking into the grass of the moor.

Tommy pulls me away.

"You're not going to give money to one of those frauds," he says. "Or maybe you think it's *you* who should be in one of those caravans?" He looks sideways at me.

"I'm genuine," I say. "I wouldn't prostitute my gift like that."

My pockets are full of petals, leaves, stems; dried, freshly-picked, multi-coloured. My wrists and neck and ankles are weighted down by jewel-hued stones, delicate crystals hanging on threads, to protect, to ease pain of heart, to open up other hearts to myself. I wear the markings of my ancestors on my sleeves.

Tommy has just completed his finals for his Psychology degree, is planning to stay on another year to do a masters.

He reckons I have "extreme identity issues." That I "over-compensate" through over-identification with a fraction of my gene pool, based on a tenuous link by family name, the colour and texture of my hair, the dark rim of my eyes.

"It's my heritage," I say, trailing heather stuck to the bottom of my plimsolls.

He points out, "but you're from East Boldon." Clever, rational Tommy. So sure of himself, of his future, of his place under heaven.

A gaggle of men in short-sleeved shirts walk past, singing "Who Ate All The Pies?" I throw out a curse, silently, in their direction. One slips up and stumbles, pulls a mate down with him into the dried up mud and grass.

There's something sinister about fairgrounds. Everyone knows this, except Tommy, who really does believe it's all about the rides and the rush. I tell him the heart of the fair is the freak show.

It's not actually called The Freak Show; of course not. Its official title is *Marvels from the Seven Continents*.

Tommy says, "but they're only five."

"Not if you count Antarctica, and two Americas."

"Five," Tommy insists. "Like the Olympic rings."

The sign is scrawled in marker-pen on thick brown cardboard. A wobbly arrow points the way to a weathered portakabin, patched up with decaying planks of wood. It's at the very back of the fair. It looks like a cowshed and indeed there are a series of dried cowpats, like stepping stones, leading all the way to the portakabin door.

"I've never seen anyone go in," I say to Tommy. He gives me a look. "Doesn't that tell you something?"

"Yes. It tells me that people aren't very curious." I remember the queues of desperate, yearning women, lined up in front of a sign that proclaims *Uncannily accurate says Deirdre Barlow, Coronation Street.* "Or at least, not about anything that takes place outside themselves."

Tommy sighs. He thinks I'm hopeless.

In the city in Spring, before the Hoppings, a woman in a confidence-building workshop says, "Complete this sentence: I am like (a fairground ride)." I try hard to visualise myself as the upwardly mobile gravity-defying Big Ben ride, but instead, I can't help myself, I imagine a hall of mirrors. I read out loud my sentence: I am like a hall of mirrors where every image is distorted. The confidence-building woman nods in a sage manner. She thinks I'm an idiot. But this is how I imagine the freak show, a hall of mirrors.

Except it's not a hall, it's a bare room with a portakabin, with one plain mirror, full-length, that doesn't distort at all.

Tommy always says my thoughts are too random. Modular, like the Hoppings, where different rides come together only to disperse ten days later. Tommy's mind is more orderly, his thinking-processes are shapely and well-connected, like fan vaulting in a cathedral. That's why he'll get a First and I'll only get a measly 2:1.

We arrive at The Bomber. It has two long arms, like a deformed windmill with a paucity of limbs, weighted at each end with people locked into seats, screaming. They travel forwards and backwards, and the arms spin on their horizontal axis as well as round the central point, so that people are held upside down, hair flowing towards the ground.

"Don't go on there," I tell Tommy, gripping his arm.

"Why not?" Tommy extricates himself from my grip.

"Because." I can't tell him I've got a strange feeling.

Tommy snorts. "Don't tell me. You've got one of your funny feelings."

"Even if I don't have endorsements from soap stars, I have to be right at some point. To be wrong all the time is against all the laws of averages."

Tommy concedes the point.

I say, "I *am* Romany."

"It doesn't count if you live in a student-share Tyneside flat in Jesmond."

He doesn't believe me. I admit I've been wrong in the past.

I don't say, like when I believed we were – would become – more than friends? But I came home and you were on the settee with that skinny bint from my Scottish poetry seminar, the one I'd already told you had been behaving like a complete bitch to me all term. And I knew that you'd meant for me to see. Or that time we were both drunk on cooking lager and we climbed into the bath and you said I had more flesh than all the girls you had ever met put together and I sobered up straight away after that but you just laughed and in the morning you had forgotten. I don't say that to him.

Instead I say, "Tommy, I'm asking you, please don't go on this ride."

"You're being silly. Of course I'm having a go."

After a pause I relent. I say, "OK. But I'm thirsty. Let's have a drink first. Do you want one?"

"Not really." He looks longingly at The Bomber.

"It won't upset your stomach. Stay here, I'll be back in a minute."

I buy one can of Dr Pepper from a chip and burger stall. I open it but I don't drink. Instead, on the walk back to Tommy I reach inside one of my gypsy-skirt pockets, pull out a miscellany of red flowers, purple stems, dried brown leaves; crush them between my fingers, slip them into his fizzy drink.

"Where's yours?" he asks, when I get back and offer him the can.

"I only bought one. I took a few sips but then I wasn't thirsty anymore."

Tommy shrugs and takes the Dr Pepper. He never refuses food or drink once it's shoved under his nose. He never gets fat either, no matter what he eats, or how much. Slim as a foxglove stem, my Tommy, pretty as belladonna.

Tommy drinks it all in one long slurp, then burps so he won't get sick on the ride. Two girls walking past giggle at the sound of him, but the smirks on their faces are good-natured rather than scornful. It helps that Tommy is good looking, dark hair flopping into his eyes like a singer he sometimes gets told he looks like, usually by naïve first years fresh from home and eager for love's brutish rutting. Tommy can do quite a lot of disgusting things in public, burp, belch, fart, and still get looked on with an affectionate, forgiving eye. Whereas I have only to bump into a stranger in the supermarket to get called a bitch.

Tommy pays for his ticket (£5) and gets strapped into The Bomber. I watch him go up and down, hands free as he goes past me waving, hair pulled down by gravity, screaming, pretending to be more frightened than he really is. The people on The Bomber go backwards and forwards, round and round, get held upside down by mechanical arms held at noon's position, poised, waiting in freefall before that stomach lurch and then back down again.

I think, but am not sure, that Tommy is starting to turn green. He does not wave as he goes past now, instead, uncharacteristically, he clutches at the safety bar that keeps him strapped into his seat. He's not screaming now. As I watch his face flash past, his lips are thin and pinched tight.

When he comes off, finally, he doesn't run and jump and

gurn in my face the way he usually does after these rides, body pumped with adrenalin. Instead he zigzags, staggers, slides on the grass towards me, hands reach out, then he stumbles at my feet. He kneels and I wonder if he is going to be sick over my trainers.

"Are you going to be sick Tommy?" He doesn't answer. I look down at him. He's turned puce. I observe him with some interest.

Tommy lies in the dirt, twitching. He is at the centre of a widening circle of people. White drool is spitting from his lips and his limbs are flailing out of time to the tinned music emanating from The Bomber. The two men selling tickets for the ride are looking distinctly uncomfortable. Someone asks, "Is he alright?" Imbecile. But I suppose it must be difficult to process what we are not expecting to see.

Later, the ambulance crew ask me if he has epilepsy.

"No," I say.

In fact, he's never had so much as a cold the whole time I've known him. He's always been super-fit, ultra-healthy.

Later still, when it's all over, a policeman asks me if Tommy used drugs.

"You don't need to cover up for him now," he says, while tears fall down my cheeks.

"I don't know. Why, do you think it was something he took?"

"Could be, could be," he murmurs.

The senior detective glances away, asks too casually, "Why did it take you so long before you called for help?"

"I thought he was just mucking about," I say between tears and intakes of breath. "Trying to spook me. He often played practical jokes. He liked being the centre of attention. You know what good looking boys are like."

The detective nods. He is overweight, tired-looking, trapped in ill-fitting clothes that I know leave marks on his skin when he takes them off at night.

"That was Tommy all over," I say, a well timed teardrop overflowing the rim of my glistening left eye. "He was always making a spectacle of himself."

"Look at me," he'd say.

Look at me.

Look at me.

There's No Place Like Home

Voyeurism is truly the last refuge of the mediocre and the dead. When I was alive, my days were spent drinking vinegar-cheap red wine while I sat and watched celebrity reality game shows on the brain-rot box, or turned the pages of glossy celebrity magazines, weekly, bi-weekly and monthly. This was my life's work, interrupted only by the necessary daily bouts of my job, intermittent sleep and unavoidable bodily functions. Resolutions – to drink less, get more exercise, learn another language, play a musical instrument, find a better job, lose weight, gain a boyfriend – were made with annual, monthly and weekly frequency, and broken daily, with little effort in either the making or the breaking. I did not record in a diary the number of chocolate croissants consumed. I did not join a gym in the first week of every January. The notion of activity merely flickered through my mind like a page in a magazine and was just as easily turned over, discarded or put aside for recycling.

Such stasis could have comfortably lasted me into old age with its attendant senior-citizen poverty, when I would then have had to share my glossy spoon-fed gossip with others of my kind: dog-eared and thumb-smeared crones who gathered in public libraries to take advantage of the free subscriptions and the central heating. If I were not especially looking forward to such a future, it would be inaccurate to suppose I was dreading it. Any attempt to wield the dowsing rod of imagination and consider what life may bring me always uncovered the same stream of thought: that it would continue much the same, for a long time, until I grew old and died.

Death was not as dramatic a change as you might have supposed. There was no transformation of personality or circumstances of either the demonic or angelic variety. I registered some surprise at finding myself still alive, as it were, after death, but this was quickly muted into an incorporeal shrug and I settled down into my after-life as if it were a sofa and I was watching yet another reality TV-show, one with no commercial breaks. I still occupied the same one-bedroom flat; I could look out through the window and the front door but I couldn't get them open, and the view was dense with fog.

Tomas was the third tenant after my early demise. The two previous usurpers – both of them women – did not appear to stay for very long, although I find it hard to gauge time accurately. It was raining when he came. Puddles formed in the wake of his dripping footsteps. He was bony, angular, with a face too long for his features. His hair was blond and thin and matted into waves so that he always looked as if he'd just come in from the rain anyway. The first time, he was genuinely wet. His meagre belongings were stuffed into two large plastic bin bags from which water ran down in funnels, and a cardboard box holding his DVDs was disintegrating into a damp sludge. He didn't look like a promising flatmate. I feared hours of listening to the techno background of Xbox games were ahead, but no. His great passion was for film.

Most of his films divided into two categories, those he played in the background for comfort – usually comedies that he had seen before – and then those he actually watched: subtitled films that required attention in order to fully understand what was happening. His first act when he crossed the threshold, (after going to the toilet), was to switch on the TV and DVD player and put on *Blithe Spirit*, so I was forced to listen to Margaret Rutherford twittering on as the medium while he unpacked his bin bags. He took out a photograph and placed it on the telly. It was his only decoration. The photo itself was rather nice: a girl – a young woman – about my age when I died, somewhere in her early 20s, dirty blonde hair, large mournful eyes, and a slight smile that curled up the edge of her lips. She was a plumper, much prettier, female version of Tomas.

One of the unexpected benefits of life after death is the ability to watch whatever you want on the television. It's only once you die that it becomes clear who the true target audience is for most programmes: us, the dead. I say us, because I cannot assume I am the only one. However, I've never seen anyone else. I'm not lonely. I have the same ersatz family and friends as before: the girls on *Next Top Model*, the housemates of *Big Brother*, the lovers on *Love Island*. I only have to focus my attention on the television for the screen to form itself into the correct pixels. Shadows and light, that's all we are, in life and death.

The only difficulty arises when one of the living decides they want to watch something else. The tenants previous to Tomas were no problem in this respect: they shared similar tastes, and even bought the same magazines, which I read while they were at work. Tomas was not so amenable a flatmate. When I wanted to watch *Next Top Model* he would put on Ingmar Bergmann. When I wanted to watch *X Factor* he would be casting his eye over a Powell and Pressburger. There were other issues too. Men are disgusting in the bathroom. I won't go into details, suffice to say he won't be challenging George Clooney in the grooming stakes. I've never been one to make much of a fuss, but what was the point in being dead if you still had to accommodate others? Tomas had to go.

I wasn't quite sure how to go about a haunting, and there was no-one I could approach for advice. There were any number of reality TV shows that took place in haunted houses, or with self-proclaimed mediums, but as a How-To guide they were pretty useless, dependent as they were on odd green lights flashing across the screen and a few Z-listers exclaiming in frightened mock-whispers "What was that noise?" followed by a scream. I began to suspect that these were not real hauntings at all. The main difficulty was that I didn't appear to have the ability to make a noise – no chance of mysterious howls in the night – except by disordering physical objects. Tomas was quite the slob, so that things often fell over on their own accord. The only way I could see to have any effect was to bring some order to his chaos. After a week, however, it became apparent that the reason Tomas was so messy was because he barely noticed his surroundings. One night I did the washing up; in the morning, he failed to notice his gleaming sink. When he was at work, I plumped up the cushions on the sofa and moved it to a more comfortable angle in front of the television. He fell asleep in it. I threw away his out of date bathroom products, and pulled his shower curtain open to prevent mould. He simply re-smeared the bathroom cabinet with toothpaste. I had a horrible feeling he might be developing the impression that his rent included the services of a cleaner.

The only option was to mess with his DVDs, the one thing he seemed to care for in the face of his indifference to clean dishes, personal hygiene, physical appearance or the arrangement of furniture. So I moved the sofa back against the wall, and in the floor space I laid out the first 20 of his DVD cases, with the discs removed and placed next to them. It looked quite pretty with them all shining up at the ceiling. He noticed that alright. Personally, if that sort of thing had happened to me when I was alive, I would have freaked. But Tomas didn't move, just stood in the doorway contemplating my artwork. It occurred to me that maybe he'd gone into shock, or was paralysed with fear, but then he bent down and started to check which films they were.

I had picked them at random, but as Tomas examined each one I could see there was a certain theme running through them: *Blithe Spirit, The Ghost and Mrs Muir, The Seventh Seal, A Tale of Two Sisters, Medium Series 1, Dead Like Me*. I hadn't meant to hammer him over the head with such clues, but coincidence had intervened. He was still too calm though. I was the one being unnerved.

"Irina?" His voice was hoarse, the first indication that he wasn't as calm as his thin face suggested. His hand went up to his straggly hair and then over his eyes. "Can it…?" he muttered, and then louder, the same name, "Irina!"

The girl in the photograph.

He left the DVDs as I had placed them for three days. I couldn't bear it any longer than that, and put them away myself. When Tomas came home that evening, he registered their absence from the floor and sat down on the sofa without taking off his coat. He had come in with a crumpled carrier bag, which he had set down by his feet. Now he reached down and took out its contents: a folded plastic board and what looked like a small library magnifying glass. I thought it might be a chess board, but when he opened it out, instead of chequered squares the cream plastic board was covered with over-stylised letters of the alphabet, numbers, and two words: "yes" and "'no". Tomas laid the board flat on the floor and knelt over it. He clasped the small magnifying glass, a circular lens set in a teardrop of teak-coloured plastic, over the board like a dowsing rod and asked out loud, "Is there anybody there?"

I was so annoyed that I dragged the glass over to the word "no".

"Typical Irina." He laughed. "Bolshy cow."

If I had ever tried to imagine life after death, then I suppose I would have imagined it with more people. A celebrity gallery, even, where I would get to meet Marilyn Monroe, Kurt Cobain, River Phoenix, Heath Ledger, James Dean and Elvis. I haven't even seen the old woman who died in the flat upstairs six months after I moved in. Irina, it transpires, was Tomas's sister. He had any number of undeleted texts from her in his phone, which he would re-read from time to time. There was nothing special in them, just ordinary messages such as: "meeting Suz at the Union Rooms 8pm, fancy a pint, sis xx?" I don't know what happened to her. Perhaps she was in a flat just like this one in another part of the city, and just as annoyed at having to share it with a man with whom she had nothing in common. Whatever. The DVD debacle, as I came to think of it, had backfired, and instead of having less Tomas in the flat, I had more. He stopped going out at the weekends. Not that he ever had much of a social life, but at least he used to go out shopping for DVDs, film magazines, and caramelised peanut bars. He started pulling sickies. His days were spent hunched over the Ouija board, calling out to Irina, asking her all sorts of questions, or on very bad days, just muttering to her in a kind of non-stop rambling confession of the petty misdemeanours all siblings commit in childhood.

I wouldn't have thought it possible for Tomas to get any thinner, but he was becoming positively skeletal. I was terrified. It was like being haunted by the living, and worse, what if he died and I was stuck with him here, fighting between Sky Living and Film Four Extra? So of course, I hid. There was no way I wanted him to think there was a ghost here, of any sort, let alone his sister. I tried to lay plans for an anti-haunting, but there isn't much you can do other than keep very quiet and try not to move anything. And not change the channel. But the more I kept quiet, the more fervent Tomas became about making contact. His desire to speak to his sister served as impetus to get him out of the waking coma he had slipped into, and so one morning when he got out of bed, instead of heading for the sitting room after his first-thing-in-the-morning micturation, he got into the shower (no, I didn't look) and had a shave. He got dressed, scraped together all the coins that had fallen into the crevices of the bed, the sofa and in a variety of pockets of unwashed trousers, and went out. I don't know why that morning rather than the one before or the one after. Perhaps he'd had a dream. I wouldn't know: I had often tried to watch his dreams, but I didn't seem to be subscribed to that channel.

Tomas came back later with a sausage roll in one hand and an A5 flyer in the other. The flyer had a phone number on it, which he called.

"Hello? Madame JoJo?"

I had a bad feeling about this.

Madame JoJo came round the next evening. In advance of her coming, Tomas had engaged in an unprecedented level of housework, cleaning the kitchen sink, scrubbing the bath, pouring bleach down the toilet. He would have done the hoovering too, if he'd had a hoover. He'd also bought three carrier-bags worth of food and drink, much of which he'd already consumed. Most astonishing of all, he ironed a shirt. A shirt with an odd 70s floral print, but I'll admit it did suit him in a funny kind of way. Not that I paid that much attention to what Tomas looked like.

The intercom buzzed at 7.30pm on the dot (I know, because Coronation Street was about to start). Madame JoJo was horribly familiar. Although her business name led one to expect a weather-beaten older woman with a headscarf and large hoop earrings, she turned out to be a woman in her late 20s, with dyed blonde hair and fake ugg boots. Her name was Joanne Jones.

"You found the place alright then?" Tomas asked.

"Yes! Actually, you won't believe this, but" she said, and I knew what was coming, "I used to live here."

"No way! When?"

"For a year, until about 3 months ago. You must have moved in shortly after I moved out. I knew as soon as you telephoned that this was going to be an important meeting."

"Wow." Tomas asked the obvious question. "Did you feel

any, er, presences when you were here?"

"I always felt that this flat had an aura. Nothing bad, but as if there was someone watching over me, you know?"

Tomas was nodding.

"So it was a good presence?"

"Oh yes. Most of them are, you know."

My arse. If I still had one.

Tomas poured them each a glass of white wine from one of the bottles he'd bought earlier and they sat down together on the sofa.

Joanne Jones was indeed the tenant before Tomas. Madame JoJo was clearly a new incarnation, for there was never any indication that Joanne was touting herself as a medium while she was here. As far as I remember, she was a temp with Office Angels. I had no particular dislike for her at the time – she read *Heat* magazine where I preferred *Look*, but we had gravitated towards the same favourites among the Big Brother household. I hadn't remembered that she had such an irritating laugh. And it was only becoming apparent to me now, as she was explaining to Tomas how she "got into" mediumship, just how much her speaking voice grated on my ethereal hearing. Plus her roots were showing through. And her skirt was too short for her plump fake-tanned thighs, which spread out like melting marmalade when she sat down.

This didn't appear to bother Tomas. In fact, the conversation kept turning more towards Joanne and less towards trying to contact his sister.

I knocked Irina's photograph off the television and onto the carpet.

Joanne spluttered on her wine, but Tomas waved a hand at her in a gesture of "it's nothing."

"The floor here is quite uneven," he said. "Things are always falling over, I think it must be the traffic vibrations from outside." He placed the photograph back on the television. I let them settle down, and then I knocked the photograph down again.

Joanne set her wineglass down on the carpet.

"I think something very important is happening here," she said. She knelt down on the carpet to peer at the fallen photograph. Her skirt hitched up a little higher.

"You're right," agreed Tomas. "Can I show you my ouija board?"

Joanne was doubtful. "Those can be very dangerous in the wrong hands. Sometimes they can call up other, less benevolent souls."

"I'm sure you know what you're doing."

"Well, if you're sure."

Tomas looked at her thighs, and nodded. "I'll get it out."

I was in a bad mood. Not only was I missing my favourite programmes, but now I had to watch Tomas making moves on a fake medium. It was painful, worse than watching George

Galloway doing his cat impersonation on Rula Lenska, and I started to think with affection of those evenings spent numb with boredom watching *The Seventh Seal*. Joanne and Tomas took it in turns to ask questions. Every question Tomas asked, I answered by spelling out the phrase, "Do not forget me." Every question Joanne asked, I answered by spelling out, "Go Away."

Joanne sat up and said, "I think your sister is having some problems letting go."

"Can you help her?" Tomas asked.

"Oh yes, I think so," she said, the little troublemaker. "But we probably need to discuss it in another environment." She invited him to the pub the next night. That next evening, Tomas didn't come home until after midnight. I could have watched anything I wanted, but I felt unfocussed and kept channel hopping without taking anything in.

The next night, Tomas didn't come home.

I threw a bit of a hissy fit. I took all of his DVDs out of their cases and put them in the wrong cases. After two days, when it became clear Tomas wasn't going to notice, I took out all the discs and scattered them, and the cases, all over the sitting room floor. Tomas came in, saw the mess, and immediately called Joanne.

"It's just as I thought," she declared, as soon as she arrived. "We need to act soon, tomorrow preferably. That will give us a little time to prepare. In the meantime, you'd better stay at my place tonight. For safety."

Tomas nodded happily. So much for "mostly benevolent souls": I was now cast in the role of malicious hag, thanks to my erstwhile co-habitant Madame JoJo. How easily Tomas betrayed his sister. I was glad Irina wasn't here to see it. Tomas left with Joanne and a bag with some underwear and shaving stuff. I tried watching the new series of *Extreme Makeover* but was too distracted, and ended up tidying away all the DVDs instead. Then I alphabetised them, first by film title, and then by director.

They didn't come back until three days later. It was a Saturday. Joanne carried a little case full of tea lights and matches, Tomas had a large red blanket. He laid the blanket down on the sitting room floor, in front of the television where Irina's photograph still perched like an abandoned altar. Joanne set the tealights on the edge of the blanket, to form a border, and lit them. Both of them slipped off their shoes and stood inside the square of light.

"Now hold my hand and close your eyes," Joanne instructed.

I sat down on the sofa and waited to see what they would do. What they did was talk. It was embarrassing. Joanne started, in a strange rolling voice that must have been her "Madame JoJo" voice:

"O Irina, we conjure thee from the land of the dead and ask you to take heed to the words of the living."

I giggled. If she really was a medium, she should have heard me, but she didn't.

"O Irina," she continued, "listen to the words of your brother."

I listened.

"Irina," Tomas started, thankfully dispensing with the declarative O. "Irina." He was having difficulty. I saw Joanne squeeze his hand a little tighter in encouragement. I stopped giggling.

"Irina, I'm so grateful that you are still watching over me. It means a lot that you have travelled so far from wherever you are, just to look after your brother. And I missed you, so I was really, really happy to find you here. But,"

There was always going to be a "but".

"I cannot allow myself to keep you here. It would be selfish. It's time for you to find peace, in the place where spirits go to rest."

And where would that be?

"And although it's going to be difficult, I will let you go. For your sake, I will get on with my life, without asking you to take care of me."

How generous.

"Be at peace. Find your rest. Do not worry about the living. I love you and I will see you again, one day."

It was worse than listening to a couple's self-penned

wedding vows.

They both opened their eyes.

"Is that it, do you think?" Tomas asked.

"Yes, you did very well. Now all we have to do is blow out the candles."

Ha. She turned and was about to kneel down and blow them out, but I got there first and extinguished them all at once. I was always good at birthday cakes when I was alive.

Joanne didn't miss a beat. "That's Irina saying goodbye."

I would have knocked over the photograph at this point, but Joanne reached over and picked it up. "Thank you Irina," she said, looking at the girl in the picture. Then she said, "I'll take this back with me. You start packing and I'll see you later." She kissed him lightly on the cheek and made a swift exit. She really was quite clever.

I suppose I could have made a fuss. Thrown a few DVDs around the room, switched on the TV and played with the dead channels a la *Poltergeist*. But I had seen the look of relief on Tomas's face when Joanne declared that Irina had said farewell.

He was packed within a couple of hours. It didn't take long because he'd been keeping the place tidy ever since he met Joanne, and had already taken some of his stuff over to hers. It was just a few clothes, and his DVDs. The television and DVD player belonged to the flat, along with all the furniture. He came back a few times over the next couple of weeks, to pick up mail. And then he was gone.

The landlord started showing others around the flat but after Tomas I didn't pay much attention, and after a while I stopped noticing when the landlord came round. I think someone else may have moved in now, because things keep getting moved around, and I hear noises. But I haven't seen anyone, although sometimes I definitely feel that there is a presence. It's like the flat has become two places laid over each other, with me in one version of it, and some unseen person occupying the other. Another strange thing is that the view outside the window is starting to clear up. The fog does seems to be thinning and I can now make out movement, like trees in the wind. Yesterday I was sure I even heard people talking just outside the window, which is very odd, because this flat is on the third floor. I might have another look at the front door, and see if I can get it open this time. Not today, though. Tomorrow, maybe. Today, I'm going to watch the last eviction on Big Brother.

Signs of the Last Days

Summer began early that year and the air grew hot and dusty. The city was all haze; cars drove through the heat like water, wavering and flickering right in front of us until we grew afraid to cross the street. Old women wore tight polyester dresses in bright floral prints, sleeveless, squeezed into the breathless fabric like sausage meat, their loose upper arms hanging out liver-spotted and fleshy. Young children cried and grew fractious. Weeds that normally flourished in the cracks of paving stones and broken walls withered and died. The city baked and cracked. The grass in our local park turned brown.

That summer, the radio played the same songs over and over – *Every breath you take, Cruel Summer, Who's that girl?* – until we could no longer tell the difference between the song lyrics and breathing. We skipped school and took the bus to the local high street, where we stole shell-shaped hairclips from Woolworths, and walked into Marks & Spencers in our old shoes and walked straight out again with bright shiny new pairs in black patent plastic, or white courts with three inch heels that got caught in the grooves on the steps of the bus home.

Once, Miri came with us.

Miri wore flat lace-up shoes, like a man's, and knee-length

socks. She was the only girl who wore her school blazer after the first week. When it was cold, she wore a white polo-neck under her shirt. When it was hot, she dispensed with the polo-neck and unbuttoned her collar, but still wore her blazer and the knee-length socks. Some of us knew Miri from primary school, and whispered to the rest that she was strict Seventh Day Adventist. On Saturdays she would go to church with her mother and two baby brothers. She wasn't allowed to eat bacon, or bacon-flavoured crisps, on Saturday or any other day.

Wednesday mornings was Swimming, when we would board a coach to the pools. We knew a girl had started bleeding if she only went swimming three Wednesdays out of every four. But Miri never went swimming at all. We couldn't imagine her in a swimming costume, revealing her legs, her arms. Some reckoned it was the swimming cap that was the problem: her hair was always so carefully pressed.

That Wednesday it was too hot, the air so heavy we couldn't breathe. We skipped the coach, walked out of the school gates, and just carried on walking. It wasn't until we were near the High Street that we realised Miri was with us. She was trailing behind, beads of sweat standing out on her forehead beneath her hairline.

"Miri, you's a bad girl now?"

She managed an uncomfortable smile and looked down at her laced-up feet.

"Take off your blazer," we commanded.

She shook her head, so we pulled it off her, arms pulled back behind her torso. But it was too hot for messing, so we dropped it on the side of the road, where she bent down to pick it up. She folded the blazer neatly into her bag and carried on walking after us.

We walked until we reached the entrance to an old cemetery. The gates were wide open and inside we could see a dusty path leading into green shade. We saw the tops of trees move gently in a breeze – a *real* breeze, not hot air blowing into our faces from the rushing traffic out of exhaust pipes. We walked through the gates.

The graves were old and overgrown except near the path, where a row of low rectangular mounds were covered in fragments of glass stone: blue, white, red. We thought, at first, that they were jewels.

"Don't be stupid," we said, when we realised they weren't. But they were pretty. We picked up handfuls and let them fall through our fingers.

"Stop it," said Miri. She was a tiny fly on a hot day, not worth the effort of swatting. We picked up more handfuls and poured them into our pockets, into our bags.

"You're stealing from the dead," said Miri.

"They won't miss them," we said. "Relax, girl."

A white woman in a filthy denim jacket rose up out of the dense foliage smothering the older headstones. A cigarette dangled from her thin fingers and her hair, matted into dreads, was the colour of harvest smoke. Miri screamed but it came out like a hiccup. The woman staggered towards us.

"Did'nae mean t' startle youse," she slurred, a can clutched in her other hand. "Ah'm just visiting my old nan, god rest her soul."

We didn't say anything.

"Got a light?" she asked.

We lit the cigarette for her. It took a few goes, because she kept swaying out of reach, and once, it fell out of her mouth onto the ground. When the flame took she raised her cigarette hand into a limp thumbs-up sign. Her creased skin edged up around her mouth.

"Cheers. You're sweethearts, all of youse."

And she disappeared down the path. We burst out laughing, and passed each other our own cigarettes, swiped from mothers and boyfriends, or bought in singles from the sweet-shop across the road from school.

"You want one?" we asked Miri.

She shook her head. We envied her refusal; it was too hot to smoke.

We walked deeper into the cemetery, where it was cooler. The trees were wide and expansive, their growth barely controlled, and we could hardly see the sky for leaves. Around us, headstones became more ornate, in the shape of crosses, angels, or open bibles. We came to a large marble memorial laid down on the ground, inscribed with the names of war dead, and we lay down on top of it, skirts rolled up, arms and legs spread open like starfish on the cool surface.

"And there will be wars, and rumours of wars."

"What?"

We raised our heads. Miri was standing a few feet away.

"Nothing," she said.

We read the names of the dead: Adams, D; Athill, D; Atkins, T; rolling down all the way through the alphabet until we got to Young, A.G; Young, C; Young, T. And an inscription: *Non Sibi Sed Patriae.*

"What's that mean?"

"Who cares? They're dead, don't need old-time words to tell us that."

Miri said, "Words is how the world was made."

"Oh shut up girl," we groaned.

A vein on Miri's left temple pulsed in the heat. The spots on her forehead stood out.

"Miri," we asked, "you ever thought about concealer?"

"Yeah, you wear make-up Miri?"

This was met with a slow, silent shake of her head.

"Let's get a little gloss on those chappy lips of yours."

We weren't bad. We wanted to be kind. Bags were delved into and cosmetics purses retrieved.

"This one, Miri. The colour will suit you."

She reached out and took the proffered tube of lipstick, eased off the lid, twisted the end, and marvelled at the scarlet that rose up. We gave her a little hand-mirror, plastic pink-backed, that gleamed roundly in her palm. Her hand tilted towards her face, and a circular spot of sunlight danced over a tree behind her. We couldn't see her face reflected: in the angles visible to us were leaves, and gravestones.

Miri stretched her lips into a strange grin and slicked the lipstick over them, in two slow passes that covered her mouth and the surrounding flesh in a pair of rectangular slabs. We screeched with laughter.

"Not like that! You even *know* the shape of your own mouth?"

But Miri wasn't listening. She stood amongst the graves, out-staring her face in the mirror, like a madwoman eyeballing children on a bus. We laughed, and laughed, until our breath ran out; and then we stopped.

Miri lowered her hand. The mirror dropped out of her palm, into the grass. She stepped forward, and we heard it crack under her heavy shoes. She walked right up to the war memorial and knelt down on it, paused, head bent so low she touched the marble with her forehead, it looked like prayer. But then she straightened her back, held the blood red lipstick over the surface and began to scrawl. She didn't even look down at her hand, she just wrote. Her handwriting was large like an infant, but the words were grown up: *In the beginning was the word and ... The wages of sin are death. Vengeance is mine ... I will bring ruin on those ruining the earth.* She scrawled until the lipstick was flat and the edge of the tube scraped the marble.

We cussed at the waste of a good lipstick.

"What you do that for?" we asked.

"The girl crazy," we said.

"And *she* the one complaining that we thief from the dead!"

It started like the edge of rain when you don't even recognise that it's raining. But then the drops fall fatter, fall heavy, fall fast, until you realise you're in a storm and it's too late to find shelter. No-one remembers who was first. We reached into our pockets, into our bags, and pulled out the small glass stones we'd taken earlier from the graves. We threw the red, blue, white, glass-hard bullets at Miri as she kneeled down on the memorial. At first she flinched and instinctively put her hands up over her face, but then she stood up, swaying. The heat of the day, so soporific earlier, now fuelled our irritation and restlessness. We pounced. Miri was lost underneath our hands and legs as we kicked and punched, still it didn't satisfy, so someone pulled at her shirt, neat buttons popping into the cemetery undergrowth, another girl tore at her skirt. We laughed at her wide girdle-like knickers and pinched bruises into her thighs and fleshy parts.

Delight: malicious, malevolent, pure. We knew the

expression our face wore, because we could see it reflected in each other, girl to girl to girl, like a living hall of mirrors. We had only one face.

Miri didn't scream or try to fight back. She clutched ineffectively at her torn shirt and skirt, simultaneously trying to shield herself from our blows. She made no sound other than the deep gasping of her breath, which made her shudder the way someone does when they've finished crying and are now trying to speak. The frenzy that overtook us was brief and as it started to dissipate we fell back, but threw sod at her, dirt lodging under our nails beneath peeling varnish as we pulled up lumps of grass and weed from the ground with our fingers. Even that became wearisome, our arms grew tired, our hands slippery with sweat. Miri had now buckled to the ground, and was a curl of scratches and torn uniform lain down on the marble memorial, framed by her smudged lipsticked words. Her body moved with the convulsions of her silent sobs.

Our own breath was heavy too and we sat or stood, utterly spent, waiting for our breathing to return to silence. We heard the crack of a dry twig behind us. The wild woman of the cemetery was standing there in her dirty denim, staring at us. It wasn't clear if she'd just arrived or if she'd been there watching us all along. "You girls," she said. We waited. "You girls..." she repeated, in her smoke-tar voice, but then she turned her head sideways as if she'd noticed something else, like a bird or a rustling tree, or else she had forgotten she was talking to us. After a while, she looked back, and noticed Miri again.

"Your friend needs a bit o' cleaning up, I reckon." She took a swig from the can she still carried and turned around and walked away.

The shame of her adult indifference was worse than if she had castigated us, threatened us with the police, or expulsion.

"Get up Miri," we said, but we said it as if we were the kind ones.

Miri didn't move, so we went over to her and gently pulled her up. She was bleeding where some of the stones had caught her skin. Her torn white blouse was streaked pink with lipstick and blood, and the strange lipstick stripes she had painted over her mouth now reached from ear to ear. Her eyes were red-rimmed, her breathing punctuated by hiccups.

We pulled off her torn school-shirt and covered her with her blazer, over her vest. We saw she was wearing a bra, but pretended not to notice. We walked her back to school, slowly because she was limping, and slipped into the toilets, where we cleaned her up at the sinks. We bathed her cuts. We combed out her hair. We washed her face like Veronica wiping the face of Jesus and lent her concealer, and smudged shadow around her eyes to balance out their bloodshot appearance.

The heat broke that afternoon. The sky grew dark so that it looked like night. From our classroom, we listened to the thunder. There was a flash of lightning over the school, another roll of thunder, and then it started to rain, sudden and heavy. In the space of half an hour it was over. The sky cleared.

Miri didn't come to class the next day nor any day after that until school broke up for the summer two weeks later. We stopped meeting up on Saturdays, and we drifted off across the city, some of us looking after younger brothers or sisters, some of us going to summer playschool, or to stay with cousins or aunts. By the time the new school year started in September, we could hardly recognise each other, our faces and bodies had become unmoulded from their familiar forms. Miri would walk past one, two, many of us at various times; in the corridor, or at the dinner queue. We heard rumours from other girls about how she was always getting into trouble; back-chatting teachers, skipping school, not wearing uniform. She was seen eating packets of bacon crisps. She click-clacked in stilettoes that exaggerated the height she had gained over the summer, swinging her bag over the shoulder of her leather jacket, while her skirt, rolled up at the waist to make it shorter, tilted from side to side over her swaying rear. She walked on without once turning to look at us, and we watched her disappear into the distance.

On Skar, and matters pertaining

The islands of Skar lie off the northern coast of Caledonia, more remote in social if not geographic terms than the Orcadian and Shetland islands to the northeast, and the Hebridean and Kildan groups in the west. Skar consists of twin islands – Skar and Karrion – connected by a natural causeway that floods with the tide, which can sometimes last for weeks. The language of the Skarlanders is a curious mix of Gaelic and Norse, reflecting the hybrid origins of this island race. A few words of Spanish and Arabic derivation are also found, particularly in their names for women. A plausible hypothesis for this has never been put forward, although it continues to be a fond subject for those on the more frivolous fringes of the Academy.

There is a third island, or more properly a stac, to the west of the twins, that rises sheer for over a thousand feet and is inhabited only by birds. It is known simply as 'the Amazon'. None of the islanders of Skar ever visit the Amazon except to mourn their dead, and in those cases where there is a body, to bring it for the birds. Skarlandic corpses are usually female – the men almost always die violent deaths, either by drowning or falling from a cliff face, and generally the body is never recovered, washed out into the Atlantic by the strange currents that surround the island. It is a rare thing to see a Skarlandic man over the age of 40. The ageing population is almost entirely made up of widows, who can, however, live well into their nineties and more. This high proportion of aged women is likely the original cause of those old Celtic and Scandinavian legends that proclaimed Skar to be the abode of witches.

Skarlanders are great climbers and vertigo is unknown, to the extent that they have no word for it. In strange contrast, they seem never to have fully come to terms with the sea, unique in an island race, and although they do build boats out of necessity, seamanship has never progressed as a skill amongst them, nor fishing, despite the rich catch of which they would always be assured. This lack of seafaring knowledge is a continuing enigma for the Academy; for we must ask, how did the Skarlanders reach the twin islands in the first place? Their mongrel Skarlandic language suggests that they are not so old a race as to have inhabited the island from an age before Skar and Karrion were sundered from either the northern tip of Caledonia or the southwest part of the Nordic continent. Even if such had been the case, clearly there must have been some not inconsiderable traffic with Caledonia or Scandinavia – presumably both – in the not too distant past. Furthermore, the dark, swarthy physiognomy of some of the populace hints at commerce with more southerly peoples well beyond our United Fair Isle of Caledonia, Cymru and Albion.

Another oddity of the Skarlandic people is that they have no visual arts to speak of, not even in their modes of dress: plain woollen garments, whose styles and mode of production have remained unchanged for centuries. This is not to say that they are entirely bereft of all artistic impulse that marks out human civilisation, for the Skarlanders are a race rich in poetry and song. Music is a particular love of Skarlanders of all generations, and great feasts of song are held several times a year, high on the cliffs of Karrion, where the plangent strains and echoes of their untamed melodies carry over the waters to be heard by the lonely crews of North Sea fishing boats, or the pleasure-boat tourists on their way to the islands of Kilda or Orkney. All Skarlanders participate in these feasts, which take place according to some ancient changing calendar or impulse of which only the islanders are aware or able to calculate. It is said that even those Skarlandic babes not yet weaned are brought by their mothers to peer over the vertiginous precipices of Karrion, where they gurgle wordlessly over the rhythm of the great churning sea below. Only the extremely aged women do not sing, but retreat into a strange, tangible silence.

Those who have heard the Skarlandic songs of the cliff festivals find it difficult to convey the beauty of the voices to those who have not experienced it; for some unfortunate individuals, it would have been better never to have heard those voices at all. Although nowhere near as common as some irresponsible, indeed we could say scaremongering, commentators have suggested, regrettable incidents have admittedly taken place. It has not been unknown for holidaymakers on island tours, unfortunate enough to be on deck when their ships have strayed into earshot of one of these irregularly timed festivals, to fall into a kind of mania upon hearing Skarlandic voices raised in song, to the extent that they have fallen overboard in an attempt to get closer to the cliffs. The victim of such a mania has no chance of survival, for it is impossible to swim in the currents around the islands. This is, it must be stressed, a rare occurrence, the risk of which does not seem to have impacted negatively on the Caledonian islands tourist trade. Quite the contrary: for some travellers, the idea that they might chance upon Karrion festival voices imparts a pleasurable *frisson* to their journey.

It is of course forbidden to land on the Skar archipelago without the explicit consent of the Academy. This injunction was created to preserve the primitive society of Skar from the contaminating influence of our modern world that would no doubt have to led to its demise; a harsh lesson learned from the destruction of isolated Balearic communities in the early twentieth century which has meant that the islands of Ibiza, Majorca and Minorca remain to this day desolate, uninhabited rocks. Despite this attempt to safeguard Skarlandic society, it is becoming increasingly clear that the island is in decline. The women of Skar are getting older, and there are fewer babies being born. Only one in every seven newborns is male; last year there were six births on the island. At the last census, the twin islands had a combined population of 203. It is estimated that the forthcoming census will reveal a drop in numbers to below 80. That is the most conservative estimate: there are others in the academy who forecast an even more catastrophic drop to below 40. In either case, given the low male birth-rate, and the relatively short lifespan of such males as there are, it is certain that the continued existence of Skarlanders in their native domicile will become untenable.

The question that is now raised in the Academy is whether the falling birth-rate in Skar – of both sexes – has any connection, however oblique, with the strange debris that began washing up on its shores some years ago, and that has now accumulated to such a fearful extent.

This odd flotsam and jetsam accumulates on the western shore of Skar, with further material skeined around the Amazon. When the first pieces began to appear, they were greeted as treasure by the islanders. Such odd bric-a-brac: a twelve-inch articulated figure of a soldier; several more soldier-figures no more than an inch in height, in a variety of uniforms and poses; a timepiece with rusted workings; a broken bowl, faded to sea-grey with barnacles and salt stains; several rectangular transparent receptacles in a number of colours, each with a small wheeled lid that may have been designed to act in the manner of striking a flint, collecting a now-gone fuel from the narrow tube that leads from the lid into the receptacle.

In the beginning, these pieces washed up at wide intervals. The timepiece came first, and was mistaken for something that might have been dropped overboard by a tourist. As is now widely known, it is a small ingenious piece, integrated into a bracelet-like strap clearly designed for a wrist. Indeed, since its discovery over twenty years ago, such a design has become so fashionable that even women now wear them, and pocket watches are seen as quite the old thing. The original is now on display at the National Technology Museum in Edinburgh's royal furlong. The pithy explanatory note accompanying the exhibited object lists its provenance, beyond its discovered location on Skar, as 'unknown' – as are some of the materials from which it has been fashioned, the materials of the small fuel receptacles and the soldier-figures. This latter category of objects comprises by far the most numerous of the debris landing on Skar's western shore. One could – almost – give credence to the view that they are the vanguard of an invading army.

Most poignant is the belief amongst some Skarlandic mothers and widows that the figures are an embodiment of their drowned menfolk, that disappearing population, whose bodies have been swept away to an unknown shore or pulled into secret crevasses in the depths of the ocean floor.

The whereabouts of the missing bodies of fallen Skarlandic men has long troubled the Academy. Skarlanders themselves do not consider it as out of the ordinary, but rather accept it as the pattern of their society. The males of that race take pride in a certain recklessness when climbing their formidable cliff-faces in search of eggs from the nests of gulls and kittiwakes, which form the main part of the

Skarlandic diet alongside a green salty root vegetable that the women cultivate on the grassy south of Skar. As mentioned previously, vertigo is unknown amongst them. We can add here that there is a pervasive, virtually monolithic, culture of bravado amongst Skarlandic males, in which fear of physical danger is not permissible. In some cases, extreme situations are actively sought out, particularly during courtship, involving daredevil acts of leaping and scrambling on precipitous edges. This is barely comprehensible: the overwhelming ratio of female to male in the Skarlandic population should, in any rational society, lead to a competition of females for the male. It is unsettling, to say the least, that the very reverse of such logic has become the firm tradition, despite the often calamitous consequences for the men.

It is well established that the currents around the bird-nesting cliffs of Skar and Karrion are pulled into that strange vortex of the North Atlantic known as the Northern Gyre. Until recently, most commentators in the Academy have assumed this fearsome Gyre is the ultimate destination of those drowned Skarlandic men, for no-one knows how deep into the ocean it whorls. It has always seemed most likely that the bodies of the unfortunate Skarlanders have been pulled down to the seabed, whether to rest in peace or tribulation is unknown: the deeps are as mysterious to us as the great heights of the celestial sphere. However, the accumulation of the strange debris on Skar has raised serious questions regarding this hypothesis, for it appears that the source of these odd figures and receptacles is none other than the Gyre itself.

This raises several questions, all of which are subject to much heated debate within the Academy. If objects can demonstrably arrive at Skar from the Gyre, then why have none of the bodies pulled into its current ever returned? Where does the Gyre lead? What has caused the influx of objects from the Gyre to Skar over the past two decades? Where do they come from? Why is this influx now increasing at such a rate? Will the rate of influx continue to increase? And crucially, will it come to an end? The Academy has now declared the western shore of Skar a zone of environmental catastrophe and it is feared that the relentless tide of objects now winding around the Amazon will erode the stac, causing it to collapse into the sea.

The scale and speed of this unfathomable disaster shoring up on Skar has allowed the promulgation of openly wild ideas to drift into the sober mainstream of the Academy. We would hesitate to rehearse them here if they had not already escaped into wider public discourse. The hypothesis that is most oft repeated concerns the projected existence of another Earth, linked to our own through the Gyre. It should be unnecessary to rebut such an outlandish proposal, if it were not for the hold the idea has taken in the imagination of the general populace. Rumours abound as to what this alternate Earth might be like. Extrapolating from our only evidence, its effluence, were such an entity to exist, it would be a pugilistic, profligate society indeed, given to creating figures of war with an excess of enthusiasm that not even our priests demand. What would this aggressive other place make of the number of dead men bleeding through to their world? This is the fear that has gripped the populace: once aware of our existence, such a warlike society cannot fail to desire an incursion into our own demesne.

For once, the priests and the Academy are at one in their response to these rumours: they are the ill-founded, ill-imagined scare stories of subversive elements, designed to frighten and unsettle the general public and overthrow the Academy. We are facing the extinction of society on Skar, this much is certain, and it is true that the Northern Gyre offers us more mystery than explanation; but it is much too big a leap for rational minds to then postulate the existence of another world, linked to ours through the most unlikely of portals; and as the priests reiterate, there is no provision made for an unknown twin planet to Earth in the sacred writings. Both religion and science, then, refute the hypothesis.

Whispers reach the Academy of an even stranger story: that the other world does exist and is in fact the original model; that we are nothing but a shadow of that planet, with little more reality than a dream. We mention it here to demonstrate how unorthodoxy to Academy doctrine inevitably leads to the ridiculous. It needs no sophistry to rebut the mutterings of subversives and madmen; patently we exist.

Adverse Camber

Either the road is very long, or you are driving very slowly, for you have plenty of time as you drive to look about, and to wonder what will happen next. The only road you know around here that is as long and straight and lonely as this, is the military road the Romans built parallel to Hadrian's Wall. So you relax, because at some point you'll reach the Robin Hood Inn, and that village with the petrol station, and you can re-orientate yourself from there. Ahead of you, through the windscreen, all that the headlights illuminate is darkness, so that you cannot see where you are going; but peering out of the side windows, you gradually manage to make out shapes and shades as you travel past.

The curve of a beak, the flick of a long reptilian tail, and as the coppice bends in the triangular breeze of your vehicle's aerodynamics (so you must be travelling at some speed, surely, although the dial is broken and you cannot be certain), you think you see an eye, much larger than you would like, glassy and cruel. It blinks, and its eyelid is a hood of thick leather. A swish, a flap of wing, and then you blink, and it's gone, a mere trick of the light, or perhaps it's better to say, a trick of the dark. You peer into your rear-view mirror to try and catch a glimpse of the fleeting image retreating, but behind you it's as blank as it is ahead, with nothing to be seen but the dark blue night.

Except, of course, for your passenger in the back seat. You try to engage him in conversation, talking to his image in the mirror.

"Dark, isn't it?" you say.

He nods, and looks out the left window. You wonder how long he's been sitting there. You check the fuel gauge, but like the speed dial, that seems to be broken too, claiming a full tank when, truth be told, you cannot remember the last time you stopped off for petrol. There is a faint smell, but you're not sure whether it's coming into the car from outside, or if it's the car itself. Some kind of burning smell, like a barbecue, dry grass or a cranky brake pedal.

"Can you smell burning?" you ask.

A faint movement of his shoulder may or may not be a shrug. He looks at you looking at him in the mirror, and turns away to face the left window again.

"How long do you think it'll take us to get there?" you ask.

"Don't you know?" he asks.

A woman in a pale dress is either standing at the roadside or walking sideways like a crab. She is keeping exact pace with you while the gorse appears to move behind her, on the left hand side of the car. In other circumstances you might stop and offer her a lift, but now the brake pedal is so far away from your foot that the time it will take you to transfer your foot from the accelerator to the brake is infinite. No matter how close your foot gets to the brake pedal, you know that distance can always be halved so that there is always some distance left; and knowing this means you will never reach it.

You are unsure, too, whether there is one woman by the roadside or a series of them, all wearing pale dresses, popping into momentary existence as you drive past. You might, even, be driving so fast that you are going backwards (and because the speed dial is broken you really cannot be sure), and the women merely after-images of women you have already passed on the road. Later, there is a point at which they vanish, but you cannot remember where or when that was, or what the women looked like, or the road behind them, or if it was just one woman after all.

Your passenger stirs in the back seat. He turns to look through the right window.

"Where are we going?" he asks.

"Don't you know?" you ask.

Later, he says, "I thought you would tell me."

"Aren't you supposed to tell me?" he asks.

Later, he says, "I think I can smell burning."

"Cold, isn't it?" you say.

You can't remember whether you were always this bad at conversation. You can't remember ever having any other conversations.

"And dark," he says.

"Is it always like this?" he asks.

"Do I know you from somewhere?" you ask.

"I know you, don't I?" you ask.

"Don't I know you?" you ask.

Later, he says, "I think that we may have met before. Yes. I think we have."

You think you can hear wings but the coppice is empty. Eventually it grows sparser, until the landscape clears out into dark open fields on either side, with low, thinning hedgerows on the edge of the road. The night is clear on both the driver and the passenger side, but still, you cannot see ahead.

Stars edge over the horizon to the left, grouped in odd constellations that you do not recognize. Later, they disappear over the horizon to the right. Later, they rise over the left horizon. You stare at the gauge for your fuel tank and it tells you that the tank is full. The road stretches on, or maybe it curves round and round in a perfect circle. You cannot tell. But the road doesn't end and you keep on driving.

You don't want to get stuck here.

The Weather in Kansas

The world came to an end on a Thursday but there was still more waiting.

It was a bit lonely at first, I suppose I can say that now, but then David came along in one of the later resurrections, much to his surprise as well as mine. I remember when he died, even though I'd been quite young at the time, and we're not really supposed to remember much of the time before. It had been on the news, and the BBC had screened his most famous film in tribute. He had died in California from a gunshot wound to the chest. Self-inflicted. His body was flown back to the UK, where he'd been buried in a Jewish Cemetery in London, so why he had been resurrected in the North of England was anyone's guess. "An act of mercy," David said, with a grim smile. At infrequent intervals he'd ask me, "Is this how you imagined it would be?" but that's a hard one to answer. I do miss the films.

I'd had some ideas – they seem a bit silly now – of how I'd like to spend eternity in the New World Order, but mostly I'd been concerned with practicalities, on how to survive the last days, to be found patiently waiting for the New Life to begin. To be found in a state of Waiting was meant to be our highest aspiration. Like the virgins of the parable, who waited for the bridegroom with their oil lamps. Some kept their lamps filled, others wasted their oil so that the light went out at the crucial moment. I kept mine filled but I suppose you could say I spilt it near the end. I had waited long enough though, and lo! The things foretold had come to pass.

David and I live in windy isolation here on this hill in Cumbria. In the old world it was called Hart Top. There's still a sign, somewhere. On a clear day you can see Scafell Pike and Blencathra, and beyond that, very occasionally, the sun setting on the Western Sea. There is a cafe at the summit of Hart Top from the before time, which David now runs after a fashion, sleeping at night in a little back room beyond the kitchen, and there is a tiny cottage a little further down that used to be inhabited by a poet. That's where I live now. Sometimes I flick through the poet's notebooks. His handwriting was terrible. I don't know what happened to him. He's not here and if he died in the before time, he hasn't come back.

We're not left alone up here. Travellers pass through, on their way to the Western Sea, sometimes individually, more often in small groups of pilgrims. Today, twelve bikers arrive. They order coffee and a full breakfast each, so I have to help David out in the kitchen.

It's funny what things get set aside. Apart from David, who is particularly meticulous about facial hair ("*I don't want to look like part of Snow White's entourage*"), I haven't seen a clean-shaven man for a few centuries now. Shaving doesn't appear to be a big feature of eternity. I suppose it's the endless round of having to go through it all every morning.

I used to feel like that about the washing up, but actually, now I'm quite grateful for any routine. Still, these bikers have the most impressive beards I've ever seen. Not the longest, but voluminous and simultaneously luxurious and grizzly; somehow, definitely, the most excessively beard-like, like these are the original beards that all other men copy.

David's a bit upset by their arrival, something you wouldn't be able to tell unless you know him. It's the way his face sets into a stare somewhere past your shoulder. I don't know what he's got against them: they don't even blink at his short stature, which is unusual. Even in this age of odd happenings, humans still judge by appearances. Perhaps we are always going to be this shallow.

"Are you alright?" I ask him in the kitchen.

"What do they want?" he asks.

"Coffee and the full monty, times twelve," I tell him.

He gives me a look I can't quite decipher.

"Not their order," he says. "What do they *want?*"

"Is this a philosophical question David?" He's fond of those.

"You have no idea, have you?" He shakes his head. He thinks he's smarter than me, but it's not really offensive, because he thinks he's pretty much smarter than most people. He probably is.

"I'll do the coffees," I tell him, and leave him to crack eggs.

When I bring out the coffee I find the men sitting round four tables they have pushed together to form one large square.

"That's right, make yourselves comfortable. It's nice to have a big group up here. Gets a bit lonely here otherwise."

They don't say anything.

"Milk?"

One of them turns his large brown eyes to my face. "Thank you," he says, and his voice is so hoarse from lack of use that I can't stop myself from gabbling on into the silence.

"It's sheeps milk not cows. Hope that's alright. You don't get many cows these days, not around here, I've never quite worked out why. But lots of sheep. You'll have seen them on the way up. Noisy daft things really, but you get quite fond of them over time. Travel far have you? We don't get to see much, me and David. Sort of stuck here really, so it's nice to get a bit of news from travellers."

There's a bit more silence, but I don't think it's because they're unfriendly. Not that I'm such a good judge of character. They just maybe haven't spoken to anyone for a long time.

"Sugar?" I ask.

"Sugar. Yes," says the sad-eyed man with the hoarse voice, except they've all got sad eyes. Sad brown eyes and long brown hair and dark oiled beards that don't have any dust on them even though they've ridden up the hill on their motorbikes, without helmets.

"You've been here a long time I think," he says, a statement not a question.

"I think so. I'm not sure. It might not have been that long." It's hard to tell up here. It got a bit easier when David arrived and I started to keep track of the number of winters that passed. But then I lost count and there didn't seem much point trying to start up again. "I guess I've been here a while."

"And your companion?"

"David? He came here after me." I look around, conspiratorial, to make sure he's not listening from the kitchen.

"I am glad he's here. But he does get in a bit of a mood sometimes. But then, don't we all?"

The man nods. He's not really listening, which is a bit harsh I think.

There's more silence. There's a kind of quietness about them that makes me think they must be tired.

"It's a bit wearying all this, sometimes," I venture.

Twelve heads turn to look at me.

"Sometimes you wonder what's going to happen next, don't you? Only natural."

"What do you think will happen next?" asks another man. Smaller than the first one, younger possibly, but again, it's hard to tell these things.

"Now, there's the question," I say. "David thinks that maybe nothing will happen, but that can't be right, can it?"

Twelve bearded men look down at their coffee. Some stir in sugar, some stir in milk.

"I mean, it's silly to think this is it. Don't you think? After all this time."

Another pause.

"Are you going to the coast then?"

"Yes," says the first man.

"Thought so. Most people who come here are on their way to the port. Taking the scenic route though, because you don't really need to come here to get there. We're not really on the way to anywhere."

The smaller man gives me a kind smile.

"Do you know why you're here?" he asks.

"Where else would I be?" I reply.

Twelve teaspoons are tinkling against the side of their mugs and the noise jangles. Isn't it silly to have nerves, after all this?

"I think I can hear your breakfasts sizzling," I lie. "Best get back to the kitchen then."

The first man nods.

"I don't think they want anything," I tell David. "Not from us, that is."

"What did they say?" he asks me.

"Not much."

David moves around the kitchen, ostentatiously flipping things in pans. He just does it to show off, or to keep himself amused. He's a good cook but I'm sure you can do half the things he does without the song and dance.

"Don't you recognise them?" he asks me.

"No," I say. "Should I?"

David shrugs. "Depends."

"On what?"

"These are done," he says. So I take out the plates, two at a time.

David has made breakfast for the two of us as well, and we take them out to the tables and sit a little way apart from the twelve men. We don't talk while we're eating and neither do they. But there's a lot of listening going on. Metal cutlery scrapes against plates, mouths chew, salt gets shaken out from a cellar, lips part with a little pop of saliva.

David asks, "Where are you going?" He asks this without looking up from his plate, as if he's not that interested, and it's just a casual question. Small talk.

"To the coast," one of them replies. A larger man, his beard slightly frazzled at the edges with a tint of grey.

"It's where most people go," I say.

"Not us," David says. "Been there before?" he asks.

"No," says the larger man, talking with his mouth full.

"Funny that. People come this way for the coast, but you don't see them on the way back."

"They must take a different route," I say.

"Perhaps," David says.

"And what will you do," he continues, "once you get to the port?"

"There will be a ship," says the smaller man.

"Yes," says the larger man.

"There will be a ship," the first man says.

There's something odd about the way they say it, as if they're not sure.

"Is that what someone told you?" I ask.

"No. Not exactly," says the larger one, spouting crumbs.

"But it's what we've been promised," says the smaller one.

"Oh, promises," David says, and jabs his fork into a lamb sausage.

"Yes. It was a promise," the first man says, and there's an air of finality to his voice that even David doesn't want to argue.

"I hope you'll have a good crossing," he says.

"Thank you."

"The weather looks like it'll hold up," I say. Sometimes you get storms, but today is a fine day, bright and cold and clear. It's an odd thing, sometimes, the weather up on this hilltop. I remember this one film in the before time that I used to watch when I was a kid. A girl and her little dog got caught up in a storm, one of those twisty ones like we get here sometimes, and ran into a house for shelter. But then the whole house got blown away, into a strange new country. Sometimes I feel like that's what's happened to me and David, only we're not in a strange country, we're in the same place we've always been. "You should get some good views on the way back down," I tell the travellers.

"This is a beautiful country," the first man says, and I want to weep because he says it like a consolation. And I know that when they go all that will be left will be the washing up. I will have to put away the plates. I will have to wipe the tables. Tonight David will mop the floor and tomorrow I will warm up the coffee pot.

The twelve men eat their breakfasts until their plates are practically clean, and they drink their coffee down to the last empty drop.

"Would you like anything else?" I ask.

Twelve heads shake in a gentle negative.

"Thank you," says the first sad-eye man. "Thank you," they all say, each in turn, to both me and to David, as they leave the cafe and get back onto their bikes. David and I come out with them and watch them as they roar down the winding slope of the road. We don't wave. I turn to look at the view. It's a clear day and you can see all the way to the Western Sea.

David goes back through the door to the cafe.

"Come on," he says. "I don't want to leave the door open. It's cold."

But I stay outside for a little while anyway, and listen to the sheep calling to each other on the hill.

Acknowledgements

'Marginalia' was first published in *Parenthesis* (Comma Press), 'Surf Scoter' in *Wonderwall* (Route), 'Maganda' in *New Voices from a Diverse Culture* (Penguin), 'Freak Show' on Pulp.net, 'Signs of the Last Days' in *Root* (IRON Press), 'On Skar, and matters pertaining' in *Structo* magazine and 'Adverse Camber' in *Ballista* magazine. Many thanks to the Editors and Publishers of the above publications.

Thanks are also due to the indefatigable Sheila Wakefield at Red Squirrel Press, Sheree Mack and Katy Massey for early encouragement through iD on Tyne, and Jim Hinks and Ra Page at Comma Press for their comments on individual stories.

About the author

Crista Ermiya was born in London to Filipino and Turkish-Cypriot parents. She grew up in Clapton, Hackney, and now lives in Newcastle upon Tyne in the North East of England with her husband and son. Crista is a winner of the Decibel Penguin Prize for Short Stories. *The Weather in Kansas* is her first book.